"Let me go."

Caitlyn flailed her arms and Judd pulled up and released her. She fell to the ground, her eyes firing blue flames at him. "You bastard."

He rested back in the saddle, staring down at her. "Is that any way to talk to a man who just saved your life?"

She stood and dusted off the back of her jeans. "You're trespassing, Judd. Get off my property." She swung her cute butt around and headed back to the hive of cattle.

She stepped in the mud without hesitation and bent to a pipe that was gushing water.

He slid from the saddle and went to help her. His head told him to ride away. This woman had hurt him more than anyone in his life.

But his heart was the traitor, urging him forward.

Dear Reader,

I'm excited about the start of a new trilogy,
THE BELLES OF TEXAS. The stories involve three
sisters with the same father but different mothers.
I've written a lot of cowboy books and I wanted to
change the scenario and write about feisty, strong
cowgirls.

I grew up on a farm/ranch and my mother knew more
about the cattle than my dad. She knew when to sell
calves, when to cull the herd and when to change
pastures. My dad always went with her judgment. So I
drew upon my years as a child watching my mother as I
planned these books.

The sisters are independent, stubborn and know what
they want. They're willing to put their hearts on the line
to protect family and each other. Maybe there's a little bit
of a cowgirl in all of us.

I hope you enjoy the Belle sisters as much as I enjoyed
creating them.

From Texas with love,

Linda Warren

P.S. It's always a pleasure to hear from readers.
You can e-mail me at Lw1508@aol.com or write me at
P.O. Box 5182, Bryan, TX 77805 or visit my
Web site at www.lindawarren.net or
www.myspace.com/authorlindawarren.
Your letters will be answered.

CAITLYN'S PRIZE
Linda Warren

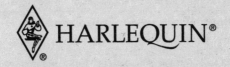

TORONTO • NEW YORK • LONDON
AMSTERDAM • PARIS • SYDNEY • HAMBURG
STOCKHOLM • ATHENS • TOKYO • MILAN • MADRID
PRAGUE • WARSAW • BUDAPEST • AUCKLAND

Recycling programs
for this product may
not exist in your area.

ISBN-13: 978-0-373-78319-9

CAITLYN'S PRIZE

Copyright © 2009 by Linda Warren.

This edition published by arrangement with Harlequin Books S.A.

® and TM are trademarks of the publisher. Trademarks indicated with ® are registered in the United States Patent and Trademark Office, the Canadian Trade Marks Office and in other countries.

www.eHarlequin.com

Printed in U.S.A.

ABOUT THE AUTHOR

Award-winning, bestselling author Linda Warren has written twenty-three books for Harlequin Superromance and Harlequin American Romance. She grew up in the farming and ranching community of Smetana, Texas, the only girl in a family of boys. She loves to write about Texas, and from time to time scenes and characters from her childhood show up in her books. Linda lives in College Station, Texas, not far from her birthplace, with her husband, Billy, and a menagerie of wild animals, from Canada geese to bobcats. Visit her Web site at www.lindawarren.net.

Books by Linda Warren

A special thanks to my editor, Kathleen Scheibling, and to Wanda Ottewell for making this series possible.

Thanks to J.O., Bobby and Chris Siegert for refreshing my memory and answering my pesky questions about ranching, cattle, windmills, oil wells and the sand and gravel business.

All errors are strictly mine.

DEDICATION

This past year has been especially difficult for me. I dedicate this book to my husband, Billy, my Sonny, who was always there to help me through it.

CHAPTER ONE

IT WAS RECKONING DAY.

Caitlyn Belle knew that with every beat of her racing heart.

She stopped at the entrance to the Southern Cross ranch and shoved the stick shift of her old Chevy truck into first. The gears protested with a grinding noise, which she ignored. Her brain cells could process only so much, and right now her full attention was on the ranch's owner, not a faulty transmission.

Once she crossed the cattle guard, there was a whole lot of reckoning waiting for her. Judd Calhoun, the man she'd jilted fourteen years ago, had requested a meeting with her. The question *why* kept jangling in her head like loose change.

Time to find out.

Reckoning or not.

She drove between the huge stone pillars that supported the decorative, arched wrought-iron sign that bore the name Southern Cross. White board fences flanked both sides of the graveled road, curling toward a massive ranch-style house with a red tile roof.

A circular drive with a magnificent horse-sculpture fountain made of limestone graced the front of the house. The place looked like something out of a magazine. The only things that signaled this was a working ranch were the corrals and barns in the distance and the white Brahman cattle that dotted the horizon.

High Five had once been like this, but not anymore. Cait felt a moment of sadness. She couldn't change the past. The future was her main concern.

The High Five, owned by the Belles, and the Southern Cross, owned by the Calhouns, were the two biggest ranches near High Cotton, Texas, a stop in the road of less than five hundred people. It had been both families' dream that someday the ranches would be one, joined by the marriage of Caitlyn, the oldest Belle daughter, and Judd, the only male Calhoun offspring.

But Caitlyn couldn't go through with it. No one understood her reasons, least of all her father, Dane Belle. He'd begged her to think about what she was doing and to reconsider. She couldn't. The rumor mill in High Cotton said she was spoiled, stubborn, but there had been a whole lot more to her decision than that.

The two families had been at odds ever since. The Calhouns prospered, while the Belles suffered financial losses one after another. Her father had passed away two months ago and High Five was barely holding on. The enormous debt Dane had incurred still angered Caitlyn. Without the royalties from the oil and gas leases, the ranch would fold. She was going to make sure that never happened.

She parked on the circular drive and took a moment to gather her wits. But her wits were scattered hither and yon, and might take more time to collect than she had. The fountain bubbled invitingly and memories knocked on the door of yesterday. She refused to open it.

Getting out, she hurried toward the huge walnut front doors and tapped the brass knocker before she lost her nerve. She studied the beautiful stained glass and saw her distorted reflection.

Maybe she should have worn makeup and a dress instead of her bare face, jeans and boots. The thought almost caused her to laugh hysterically. Judd Calhoun was not going to notice how she looked. This was business. It certainly wasn't personal. Personal feelings had taken a hike when she'd said, "I can't marry you."

Brenda Sue Beecham swung open the door. "Oh, Caitlyn, you're right on time."

Brenda Sue, a bleached blonde, had more curves than Harper's Road and was known for her friendly disposition. In high school she'd been called B.S. for obvious reasons. No one could B.S. like Brenda Sue. Her mouth was going at all times.

After a failed marriage, she was back home, living with her parents and working as a secretary in the Southern Cross office. There were very few jobs for women in High Cotton, and Cait could only imagine how Brenda Sue had gotten this one. But she shouldn't be catty. Brenda Sue's dad, Harvey, had worked on the Southern Cross for years before he retired because of a bad back. Cait felt sure he'd asked for Judd's help on her behalf.

"Come this way. Judd should be here any minute. You know how he loves his horses. Oh, what am I saying?" Brenda Sue gave a forced laugh. "You know everything about Judd. Sometimes I forget that, with you being such a stick-in-the-mud and all. Now, I don't mean that in an offensive way. You've just always been rather…you know…"

Caitlyn followed her into Judd's study, thinking that yellow hair would make a good dust mop. She pushed the thought aside. Brenda Sue and her endless digs and infinite "you know's" were the least of her worries.

"Judd will be right with you. I have to get back to the office. I help out in the house every now and then, you know. Gosh, it's good seeing you, Caitlyn." With that, Brenda Sue closed the door and disappeared.

Caitlyn hadn't said one word. She didn't need to. Brenda Sue was a one-woman show, no participation required. How did Judd put up with that airhead? But he was a man and probably enjoyed looking at her cleavage. Caitlyn didn't want to think about what else might be between them.

She took a seat in a burgundy leather wingback chair facing the enormous mahogany desk. Vibrant polished wood surrounded her. A man's room, she thought. There were no family photos, just framed pictures of prize Brahman bulls and thoroughbred horses, along with several bull and horse sculptures. A magnificent one sat on his desk, a smaller version of the one in the fountain. The stallion stood on his hind legs, his mane flowing in the wind as his front feet pawed the air.

If her nerves weren't hog-tied into knots, she'd take a closer look. Right now she had to focus on the next few minutes. She crossed her legs and tried to relax. It was only a meeting.

After fourteen years.

The knots grew tighter.

She touched her hair in a nervous gesture. After

brushing it until her arms ached, she couldn't decide whether to wear it up or down. Judd had liked it loose and flowing, so she'd weaved it into a French braid, as usual. It hung down her back and conveniently kept her hair out of her face.

She recrossed her legs and stared in horror at the horse crap on her boots. *Damn. Damn. Damn!* But when you ran a working ranch it was hard not to step in it every now and then.

Tissues in a brass holder on the desk caught her attention. Just what she needed. As she started to rise, the door opened and Judd strolled in with Frank Gaston, her father's attorney. Her butt hit the leather with a swooshing sound, but Judd didn't seem to notice. He didn't even look at her, though the lawyer nodded in her direction.

Judd sank into his chair, placing a folder on the desk in front of him. He was a big man with an even bigger presence. His hair was dark brown, his eyes darker. She'd once called them "midnight magic." Their color rivaled the darkest night, and magic was what she'd felt when he'd looked at her.

Oh, God! She'd been so naive.

The leather protested as she shifted uncomfortably. Judd had changed very little over the years. He'd been at her father's funeral, but had never gotten within twenty feet of her. She'd seen him every now and then when she was at the general store or the gas station in High Cotton, but he'd always ignored her.

As he did now.

She'd never been this close before, though, breathing the same air, occupying the same space. There were gray strands at his temples, but they only added to his appeal. A white shirt stretched across his shoulders. Had they always been that wide?

Reality check. Something serious was going on and it required her undivided attention. What was Frank doing here?

As she watched, Judd opened the folder and laid a document on the desk in front of her.

"Two months before your father died, he sold me High Five's oil and gas royalties."

Everything in the room seemed to sway. Cait's fingers pressed into the leather and she felt its texture, its softness, its support, yet it felt unreal. The expression on Judd's face, though, was as real as it got.

Something was stuck in her throat. "Excuse me?" she managed to ask.

"Are you hard of hearing?" He looked at her then, his dark eyes nailing her like barbed wire to a post, hard, sure and without mercy.

"Of course not." She wouldn't let him get to her.

She sprang to her feet, wanting answers. "I don't believe it. My father wouldn't do that to us."

"It's true, Caitlyn. I'm sorry," Frank said, a touch of sadness in his voice.

Judd poked the document with one finger. "Read it. The fifteenth will be your last check."

Grabbing the document, she sat down to see this debacle with her own eyes. She had to. Her knees were shaking. As she read, the shaking spread to her whole body. It was true. Her father's bold signature leaped out at her, sealing her fate and the fate of High Five.

How could he?

Judd Calhoun had found his revenge.

She was lost somewhere between feeling like a nineteen-year-old girl with her head in the clouds and a woman of thirty-three with her feet planted firmly on the ground. Shaky ground. What happened next? The adult Caitlyn should know, but she didn't.

Judd did, and she was very aware of that as she heard his strong, confident voice. "Dane worried about the welfare of his daughters and his mother."

"So he sold everything that was keeping us solvent. Why?" She fired the question at him with all the anger she was feeling.

"Gambling debts. He didn't want those people coming after you or your grandmother."

"So he leaves us with nothing?"

"You have the ranch."

She stood on her less-than-stable legs, but she would not show one sign of weakness to this man. He had somehow finagled her father into doing this. That was the only explanation.

Judd pulled another paper from the folder. "There was nothing he could do about the gambling debts but pay them. He felt, though, that he should made arrangements for you, your sisters and your grandmother. I agreed to honor them as best as I could."

That was her father. He was of the older generation and believed a woman had to be taken care of. That her place was in the home, kitchen or bed. Daughters were pampered and spoiled and did what they were told, like marrying a man of their father's choosing.

Caitlyn had lived with that mindset all her life. She had defied it once, to her regret.

Pushing those thoughts away, she concentrated on what Judd had said. *Agreed to what?*

"What are you talking about?"

"With his enormous debt, Dane had very few options, and he asked for my help." The rancher paused and picked up a gold pen, twirling it between his fingers. "Dane was also very aware of your stubborn, independent streak."

She stiffened. "So?" As if she wasn't reminded of it every freakin' day of her life.

"Here's Dane's deal…." His dark eyes swept over her. "If the ranch is not making a profit within six months, you will sell High Five to me at a fair market price."

"What!" His words hit her in the chest like a shot of her dad's Tennessee whiskey.

"Still have that hearing problem?"

She ignored the sarcastic remark. "You can't be serious."

"It's true," the lawyer interjected.

"Shut up, Frank." She pointed a finger at him. "What are you doing here? You're the Belles' attorney. Shouldn't you be on my side?"

"Caitlyn…"

Ignoring her outburst, Judd read from the paper in front of him. "'I'm giving Caitlyn the option to operate High Five or sell. This decision is hers, not Madison's nor Skylar's. It is my wish, though, that she consult with her sisters. To die with a clear conscience, I have to give Caitlyn a chance. But if the ranch continues to decline six months after my death, then High Five ranch and all its entities will be sold to Judd Calhoun. Dorothea Belle will continue to live on the property as long as she lives.'"

Caitlyn was speechless, completely speechless.

Her father, in his antiquated thinking, had given Judd a golden opportunity to exact his revenge. But she would not give in so easily. She would not fail.

"I...I think I'll go and let you two sort this out." The attorney glanced at her. "If you need anything, Caitlyn, just call."

"Yeah, right."

Frank shrugged and walked out.

She looked straight at Judd, her eyes unwavering. "You think you've won, don't you?"

He leaned back in his chair, the cotton fabric of his shirt stretching taut across his chest. "Yes, I've won. But knowing you, I'm sure you'll flounder along for six months. In the end I will take everything you love."

Her heart fell to her boots and her words tangled in the remnants of her shattered pride.

"Nothing to say?" he mocked.

"I think you've said it all, Judd. If you're waiting for me to beg, I'd advise you to take a breath, because it's going to be a long wait."

He lifted an eyebrow. "Beg, Caitlyn? For what?"

"Go to hell."

He shrugged. "Thanks to you, I've been there, and I'm not planning a return trip."

"What do you want from me?"

"Nothing. Absolutely nothing."

She swallowed. "Then this meeting is over."

"Not quite. I take it you are planning to operate High Five."

"You got it."

"Your sisters have to be informed of this development. Do you want to do the honors or should I?"

"I will speak to my sisters. We do not need your interference."

"Fine." He rested a forearm on the desk, his eyes holding hers. "Give it up, Caitlyn. You can't win this. Even Dane knew that. Sell now and save yourself the aggravation."

"You are not God, Judd, and you can't control people's lives."

"Control?" His laugh bruised her senses. "I never said anything about control. I'm helping a friend. Out of respect for your father, I've agreed to this arrangement and I will not go back on my word."

Respect? He didn't know the meaning of the word.

"You're a conniving bastard, Judd. I don't know how you got my father to agree to this."

"Dane came looking for me, not the other way around." He spoke calmly, but she couldn't help but note the curl in his lip.

"And you were there, eager to oblige."

He suddenly stood, and instinctively, she took a step backward. "I will own High Five and I will take great pleasure in taking it from you."

She held her head high. "I've often thought you were heartless, sort of like the Tin Man from *The Wizard of Oz,* except he *wanted* a heart. You, Judd, are lost forever. May God have mercy on your conniving soul."

"I had a heart but you ripped it out by the roots." The glimmer in his eyes was the only sign his emotions were involved. "This is reckoning day. I'm taking it all. It's just a matter of time. I see it as sweet justice."

She walked out of the room with only her dignity, which didn't feel like much. Stoically, she marched to the front door. On the silk Persian rug, she paused and wiped the crap from her boots.

Now that was sweet justice.

CHAPTER TWO

"YOU CAN'T STOP WATCHING her, can you?"

Judd tensed, but his eyes never left Caitlyn as she jumped into her truck and raced down the driveway, tires squealing. Fourteen years and she was still the same—breathtakingly beautiful with Hollywood curves, glossy black hair and a smooth olive complexion.

But it was her forget-me-not-blue eyes that always got him. They reminded him of crystal marbles his grandfather had once given him: bright, shiny and irresistible. He still owned them, tucked away in a box somewhere, but he'd long ago found that Caitlyn wasn't a thing to be possessed.

He turned from the window to face his mother. "Did you need something?"

Renee motioned over her shoulder. "I just saw Caitlyn leave."

"Yes."

"Then you told her?"

"Yes."

"Why aren't you smiling? Why aren't you happy?"

He blew out a breath. "I don't really want to get into this."

"Well, sorry. I do." His mother walked farther into the room, flaunting her usual you'd-better-listen stance. As a kid, he'd hated that tone in her voice. He wasn't crazy about it now.

"I'm not in the mood."

Renee placed her hands on her hips. In her late sixties, she was an active woman. After Judd's dad's death, shopping had become her favorite exercise and pastime. She never interfered in Judd's life and he liked it that way.

Of course, she'd never been a big part of his life. Judd had been five when she'd left Jack Calhoun and him. Judd then had the stepmother from hell.

After that marriage fell apart, his parents had miraculously reconnected, remarrying when Judd was twelve. By then there was a gulf between him and his mother that couldn't be bridged.

"From the tires squealing on our driveway, I assume she didn't receive the news well. But what woman would? You take her livelihood away from her and—"

"I did not take it." He tried to control his voice, but the words came out too loud. "Her father sold it."

"Why couldn't you have worked out a loan so payments could have been made? That way Caitlyn would have had a fighting chance."

"Why should I care about giving that woman a fighting chance?"

"Because—" his mother lifted an eyebrow that said she knew him better than he thought "—in fourteen years I've lost track of the number of women you've gone through to forget Caitlyn. I thought Deanna was the one, but the next thing I knew you weren't seeing her anymore." Renee took a step closer. "You haven't forgotten Caitlyn, so why not admit it and try to make this work?"

"Mom, you know nothing about this. You have no idea how much money Dane owed."

"It couldn't have been that much."

"Try six hundred fifty-two thousand dollars."

"Oh, my God!" Renee clutched her chest. "How could he gamble away that much money?"

"It's easy when you're losing."

The lines on his mom's forehead deepened. "Are the oil and gas royalties worth that much?"

"Yes. In a few years I'll recoup my investment. That is, if oil and gas prices don't drop. It's a gamble."

"So in a way you're doing a nice thing?"

He hooked his thumbs into his jeans pockets. "What?"

"If you hadn't paid off Dane's gambling debts, those people would have come looking for Caitlyn, her sisters and Dorie."

He rocked back on his heels. "Yep."

"So you did a good thing?"

"Ah, Mom. You have to see some good in me, don't you?"

"As a mother, I know there's good in you."

"Not this time." He walked to his desk with sure steps. "I was glad Dane asked for my help. As a neighbor, I would never have said no. As the man his daughter jilted, I was more than eager to oblige. I'm going to take Caitlyn down hard. She will beg me for mercy before this is over."

"Son, son." Renee clicked her tongue. "It's been fourteen years. Just let it go."

"I can't." He raked his fingers through his hair. "She destroyed everything I believed about relationships and trust. I'm thirty-six years old and should have a family. Caitlyn Belle will pay for what she did to me. And it's only just starting."

"Why, son? Why do you need this revenge?"

"I don't have to justify my actions."

"You can't even see the forest for the trees."

He frowned. "What does that mean?"

"It means Caitlyn loved you, but you pushed too hard and so did Dane. She was nineteen years old and all she wanted was to finish college, to be young and have fun. But neither you nor Dane would listen to her wishes. Y'all had to control her every move, and look what happened. If you had given her the time she'd wanted, you'd be married today."

"Loved me?" His jaw clenched. "Why do women have to always drag out the *L* word? It was a business arrangement solely."

"A pity no one mentioned that to Caitlyn."

"She couldn't handle it. She was weak."

Renee gave a laugh that grated on his nerves. "Weak? Caitlyn Belle? Oh, son, you're in for a rude awakening."

"Mom, just drop it."

But his mother never listened to him. "You can't see Caitlyn as a person. All you see is a woman who has to be controlled. You get that from Jack. But Caitlyn proved she can't be controlled, not by you and not by her father."

His eyes narrowed. "This doesn't concern you."

Renee waved a hand. "You sound just like your dad. He thought I needed to be told what to do. And I was to overlook his little infidelities. I couldn't, so I walked away and lost my son."

"I don't want to go over this again." Judd had heard the story so many times it was burned like a brand into his brain.

"He said he wasn't cheating on me with that

bitch, Blanche, but he was lying. As soon as the divorce was final, he married her."

"You left a five-year-old kid behind." Judd couldn't keep the accusation out of his voice.

She brushed back her blond hair, pain evident in her green eyes, pain he didn't want to see. But it was hard to ignore. "I had no choice. I couldn't continue to take that type of humiliation, but I never planned to lose my son. Jack had the money to make sure I stayed away from you."

"Mom, it's over, and you and Dad had twenty years together before his death."

"Yes, and we learned from our mistakes. Jack didn't cheat again. At least, not to my knowledge." She gazed at Judd. "You were the casualty of our mistakes. Do you remember what you did when your father brought me back here?"

He stared at the horse sculpture on his desk, not willing to speak.

"You walked out of the room and wouldn't say a word to me. That hurt. I cried and cried. Your father said you'd come around. It took a solid year before you accepted me back into your life."

Back then he couldn't understand how a mother could leave her only child. He still didn't, but she was his mom....

"Sometimes I don't think you've ever forgiven

me, or that you can forgive anyone. That's my fault and—"

"This trip down memory lane is over. I'm going to check on the cowboys."

"Dear son, listen to me. I was weak, but Caitlyn Belle is not. She will come back fighting. I've known her all her life and she will not bow easily. Be careful you're not the one who ends up begging."

"Mom…"

"I've said enough." She raised a hand. "I'm not arguing with you. I came to tell you that if you don't get rid of Brenda Sue, I'm going to strangle her."

"Just don't listen to her."

"Not listen to her? I'd have to be stone deaf not to. Her voice rivals nails on a chalkboard. The woman never shuts up."

"I'll handle it."

"If you don't, I'm buying a gun."

"Okay, okay." He strolled from the room, headed for the back door and freedom from his mother's words.

And freedom from the shattered look in Caitlyn's blue forget-me-not eyes.

CAITLYN SLAMMED ON HER brakes at the barn, causing dust to blanket the truck. Unheeding, she jumped out and ran for the corral, whistling sharply.

Whiskey Red, a prize thoroughbred, her father's

last gift to her, trotted into the open corral. Cait hurried into the barn and Red followed. Within minutes, she had her saddled.

Cooper Yates and Rufus Johns, her only cowhands, came out of the tack room. "Hey, Cait, what are you doing?" Coop asked. "We just checked the herd."

She swung into the saddle. "I'll catch you later." Kneeing Red, she bolted for fresh air.

"Hey, what's wrong?" Coop shouted after her.

She didn't pause. Red's hooves kicked up dirt as they picked up speed, moving faster and faster. If she was lucky, maybe she could outrun the pain in her chest.

Thirty minutes later, she lay in the green grass along Crooked Creek, her body soaked with sweat, her heart bounding off the walls of her lungs.

She sucked in a much needed breath and stared up at the bright May sky. The temperature was in the upper eighties, a perfect day.

A squeak of a laugh left her throat. Perfect? Far from it.

Your father sold me your oil and gas royalties.

Now what should she do?

I'm taking it all. It's just a matter of time.

Not as long as she had breath in her body.

She sat up and stared at the plum trees growing close to the creek, dried dewberry vines nestled beneath them. She and her sisters often got sick from eating too many sweet plums in the summer, and they'd gotten drunk a time or two sneaking Etta's dewberry wine.

Memories. High Five. A piece of her childhood. Her life.

It seemed as if her father had reached out from the grave to try and still control her. He'd never understood her need to be a person in her own right and not a trophy on some man's arm.

The fight for independence probably began when she was small. Her great-grandfather, Elias Cotton, had had three daughters, and it was a woeful happenstance that God had given him daughters instead of sons to carry on the tradition of High Five.

Dorothea, Caitlyn's grandmother, had married Bartholomew Belle. Bart eventually bought out the sisters, and he and Dorie had run the ranch. After several miscarriages, they were blessed with a boy, Dane. All was aligned in the heavens. At last there was a son.

But once again fate struck. Dane had the misfortune to produce daughters. It wasn't for lack of trying. Dane and Meredith, Caitlyn's mother, had been high school sweethearts. They broke up when Dane went off to college. Years later they met again and married, but it wasn't meant to be. Meredith died giving birth to Caitlyn.

He didn't grieve for long. Six months later he'd married Audrey, but again the marriage didn't last. Audrey was very religious and didn't take to Dane's gambling trips to Vegas and Atlantic City, or to his weekly poker games with his buddies. A year later she moved out with her newborn daughter, Madison.

Dane met Julia, Skylar's mother, in Vegas, and felt he'd finally met the woman for him. Julia was from a Kentucky horse family, so it had to be a match made in heaven. It wasn't. Although Julia knew Dane's bad habits, she didn't enjoy living with them on a daily basis. After two years, she'd packed her things, including her baby daughter, and left.

Three wives. Two divorces. And three daughters, all with different mothers. After the third wife, Dane gave up and accepted his fate. Without sons, High Five was doomed.

Cait had heard that all her life and didn't understand it. She'd told her father many times that she could run High Five as well as any man. That always brought on a sermon about how a woman's place was in the home, producing heirs.

That stung like a rope burn. But nothing had ever changed her father's thinking.

Then she'd fallen hard for Judd, to the point that all she could see was his dark eyes, all she could feel was excitement when he looked at her. He was three years older, more experienced and more man than she'd ever met before.

Judd was popular in school, but he never glanced her way. Then one summer Renee threw a party and the Belle daughters were invited. Judd asked her to dance and Caitlyn thought she was in heaven.

After that, they met often, and before long heated kisses were taking her places she'd never been before. She was so in love that she never questioned Judd's love or his attention.

He had a power about him that frightened and attracted her at the same time. When she was around him she couldn't think. All she could do was feel.

And that caused her to fall right into her father's plan. Marrying Judd would unite two powerful ranching families, and High Five would continue to prosper.

Cait was prepared to fulfill her duty. She loved Judd and wanted to spend her life with him. Her first year in college was fun, but nothing was more exciting than rushing home to spend a weekend in his arms. It was bliss. It was perfect.

Then Dane had said there was no need for her to return to school in the fall, that doing so would be a waste of money. She needed to focus on Judd, a home and babies. They'd had words, and she'd run to Judd, wanting him to take her side.

But he hadn't. He didn't understand her viewpoint. Why *wouldn't* she want to think about a home for them and babies? he'd practically shouted. That's what a married woman should want.

In that instant Cait saw her future. She would be like his mother, Renee, ruled by her domineering husband. She would decorate his home, serve his dinner guests, warm his bed and produce children. As Judd's trophy wife, she would want for nothing. Except being treated as an equal.

Caitlyn made the toughest decision of her life in a heartbeat. Taking off her engagement ring, she'd said, "I can't marry you. I can't marry a man who doesn't respect me as a woman."

She waited for the magic words, his profession of love and respect, but they never came. He slipped her beautiful ring into his jeans pocket and walked out of the room. Her heart broke, but she held it all inside.

Her father wouldn't speak to her for six months. Judd spoke to her for the first time today. But she'd gotten that education and she'd traveled. In the end, it brought her home to High Five.

Her grandfather had passed on and Gran had grown older. Cait was needed at home. Her father was gambling heavily and the ranch was neglected and in disrepair.

Cait had a degree in agriculture management and

worked her butt off to keep High Five afloat, but her father's debts were slowly taking them under.

Then they got the news: Dane had lung cancer and was given mere weeks to live. Cait was blindsided by grief, love and anger. Through it all she was determined to prove to him she could be the son he'd always wanted.

Sadly, he never saw her as a competent woman and rancher—only a beautiful daughter who needed a husband.

Lying in the grass, remembering, Caitlyn glanced toward the sky. "You never gave me a chance. And now…"

Tears stung the back of her eyes, but she refused to shed a single one. No one was taking High Five, especially not Judd.

Reaching for Red's reins, she stood. In a flash, she was headed back to the ranch. She had to call her sisters. Maybe together they could save their home.

But the ranch wasn't Madison's or Skylar's home. They'd been raised by their mothers, and spent only summers and a week at Christmas here. Cait had always looked forward to those times. Back then money hadn't been a problem and their father had spoiled them terribly, giving them anything they'd wanted. But their best times had been just being together as sisters, racing their horses and exploring all the special places on the

High Five ranch. It was always sad when the others left to return home for school in the fall.

For Caitlyn, the ranch had always been her home.

And always would be.

She glanced east to the Southern Cross.

Cait knew she had a fight on her hands, the biggest one of her life. There was no room for error, no room for losing.

And no room for feminine emotion.

CHAPTER THREE

CAITLYN RODE INTO the barn, feeling more determined than ever. Judd Calhoun would not take everything she loved.

As she unsaddled Red, it crossed her mind that she had once loved Judd. And if a psychologist chiseled through the stubborn layers of pride encased around her heart, a flicker of love might still be there. But Judd had just killed whatever remaining emotion she had ever felt for him. Guilt, her constant companion for years, had just vanished.

Now she was fighting mad.

"Hey, where did you take off to?" Cooper asked, walking into the barn, with Rufus a step behind him.

Her cowhands were outcasts, both of them ex-cons who worked cheap. She trusted them with her life.

Cooper Yates was bad to the bone—that's what people in High Cotton said about him. He'd had a nightmarish childhood, with a father who beat him regularly. In his teens he'd been in and out of juvenile hall.

Coop had been a year ahead of her in school and she'd always liked him. They were friends, sharing a love of horses.

After high school, Coop worked on several horse farms, determined to stay out of trouble. But trouble always seemed to follow him. When he'd hired on at an operation in Weatherford, Texas, several thoroughbred horses died unexpectedly. An investigation determined that the pesticide mixed with the feed to kill weevils had been incorrectly applied.

The owner pointed the finger at Coop. They'd gotten into a fight and the owner had filed charges. Cooper was arrested, tried and convicted. He'd spent six months in a Huntsville prison.

When Caitlyn heard the news, she was convinced Coop was innocent. There was nothing he didn't know about horses or their feed. She'd been proved right. The cover-up soon unraveled. The owner had mixed the feed and had used Coop as a scapegoat. Her friend was released, but the damage had been done. No one would hire him.

Caitlyn had urged her father to take a chance on Coop. He'd been working on High Five for three years now.

Rufus, the husband of Etta, their housekeeper,

was now in his seventies. Years ago he'd been in a bar with friends when he saw a guy slap his girlfriend and slam her against the wall. Rufus pulled him off her and the man took a swing at him. Rufus ducked and managed to swing back, hard. The man went down and out—for good. His head hit a table and that was it.

Rufus had been tried and convicted. He'd spent three years in a Huntsville prison for involuntary manslaughter. When he was released, he came home to Etta and High Five. They were a part of the Belle extended family.

Cait threw Red's saddle over a sawhorse, then pushed back her hat. "I have a heap of problems, guys."

"What happened?" Coop asked. He was always the protective one.

She figured honesty was the best policy, so she told them the news.

"Shit," Rufus said, and quickly caught himself. "Sorry, Miss Caitlyn. Didn't mean to curse. It just slipped out."

"Don't worry, Ru. I'll be doing a lot of that in the days to come." She took a breath. "I don't know how much I'll be able to pay you, so it's up to you whether you go or stay."

"I'm staying," Coop replied without hesitation. "I'm here until Judd forces us out."

Rufus rubbed his face in thought. "I go where my Etta goes, and she ain't leaving High Five or Miss Dorie. I'm staying, too."

"Thanks, guys. Now I have to go tell Gran." Cait had had no doubt about the men staying. They were close. They were family.

"We're going to fix that fence in the northeast pasture," Coop said. "I guess we now have to play nice with the lofty Calhouns."

A smile touched her lips for the first time all day. "We're going to play, but I'm not thinking nice."

Coop grinned and it softened the harshness she often saw on his face.

She waved toward her horse. "Would you please rub down Red and feed her? I have to see Gran."

"You're gonna let me take care of Red?" One of Coop's eyebrows shot to the brim of his worn Stetson. "Did you hear that, Ru?"

"Yes, siree, I did."

She placed her hands on her hips. "Okay, I don't like other people taking care of my horse, so what?"

Cooper bowed from the waist. "I'll treat her with the utmost care, ma'am."

She shook her head and walked toward the house. The two-story wood-frame dwelling wasn't as fancy as the Calhoun spread. John Cotton, her great-great-grandfather, who'd settled High Cotton with Will Calhoun in the late 1800s, had had simpler taste.

The exterior was weatherboard siding that desperately needed a coat of paint. The hip roof sported four chimneys, but since Grandfather Bart had installed central air and heat, they were rarely used.

Brick piers supported Doric half columns along three sides of the wraparound porch. A slat-wood balustrade enclosed the porch with a decorative touch. Black plantation shutters added another touch, as did the beveled glass door that had been there since the house was built.

In the summers Cait and her sisters used to sleep out on the porch in sleeping bags, laughing and sharing secrets. What she had to share now wasn't going to be easy.

She picked up her stride and breezed through the back veranda into the kitchen. Etta was at the stove, stirring something in a pot.

"Where's Gran?"

"In her room." Etta always seemed to have a spoon in her hand, and she waved it now. "I'm almost afraid to go up there." The housekeeper was tiny and spry, with short gray hair, a loyal and honest woman with a heart of gold. Cait had never met a better person.

Etta was fiercely loyal to Dorie, and worried about her. Since her son's death, Dorie tended to live in a world removed from reality. As kids, playing make-believe with Gran had been a favorite pastime for Caitlyn and her sisters. But lately it had gotten out of hand.

"What is she doing?" Cait asked.

"She had me help her get that old trunk out of the attic. She was pulling clothes out of it when I came down to start supper. We're having stew and cornbread."

"Etta…" Cait sighed. "Neither you nor Gran are to pull trunks out of the attic. I'll do it or Coop will."

"She was in a hurry, and you know how Miss Dorie is."

"Yes." Cait turned toward the stairs in the big kitchen. "I'll go talk to her."

CAIT KNOCKED ON her grandmother's door, stepping into the room when she heard her call, "Come in." Then she stopped and stared.

Gran stood in front of a full-length mirror, in a dress from the 1930s. It fit her slim figure perfectly. She wore heels and a jaunty hat that were also of that era.

"Gran, what are you doing?"

"'I've been betrayed so often by tomorrows, I don't dare promise them.'"

Cait blinked. That made no sense. Though it kinda, sorta exemplified their situation, she thought.

"Remember that line, baby?" Gran primped in front of the mirror, turning this way and that way.

"No, I don't." Cait was thirty-three and her grandmother still called her "baby." She wondered if Gran would ever see her as an adult.

"Bette Davis." Dorie whirled to face her. "As Joyce Heath in *Dangerous*. Let's play movies of the thirties."

"I really need to talk to you."

"Oh, posh." Gran knelt at the trunk, pulling out more clothes. She held up a white blouse with a big bow. "I know you remember this line. 'Fasten your seat belts. It's going to be a bumpy night.'"

Cait could say that was apt, but decided to leave her grandmother with her playful memories for the moment. Cait was worried whether Gran was ever going to be able to cope with her son's death. Soon, though, she was going to have to face facts. Cait hoped to make it as easy as possible.

She hurried down the wooden staircase and across the wide plank floors to her study. She had to call her sisters. Since Cait was in charge of their inheritance, they depended on her to make decisions that would benefit them. How did she tell them they wouldn't be receiving any more checks? *By being honest.*

She called Madison first. Their middle sister was easy—that's what she and Skylar often said.

Not easy in the sexual sense, but with her emotions. Madison was easygoing, loving, compassionate, and felt other people's pain. Cait and Sky often played on Maddie's sensitive nature because they knew she would never do anything to hurt or disappoint them. Cait was counting on her understanding today.

Madison answered on the second ring.

"Maddie, it's Cait."

"Hi, big sister. What's going on? Is there a ranch crisis?"

It was the opening Caitlyn needed. "Yes." She told her about her meeting with Judd.

There was a long pause on the other end. "Cait, I need that money. I depend on it."

Cait was taken aback. This didn't sound like her easy, understanding sister.

"I'm sorry, but it's gone."

"Can't you do something?"

Cait heard the desperation in her voice. "You need to come home so we can discuss this."

"I… I can't."

"Why not?"

"I just can't, okay?"

"Maddie, we need to discuss our options face-to-face. That's all I know to do."

There was another long pause.

"I'll try to get the next flight out of Philadelphia. I'll let you know."

"Good. I can't wait to see you."

"Cait…"

"What?"

"Nothing. We'll talk when I get there."

Cait hung up, knowing something was going on with Maddie. But what? She'd find out soon enough.

Sadly, as they grew older, the sisters spent less and less time together. Maddie had come home when their father became ill, and had stayed until he died. Before that Cait hadn't seen her in three years.

Maybe they could reconnect and become family again. There was that hope, but she knew her sisters would pressure her to sell. She closed her eyes briefly, realizing she was facing the biggest fight of her life. And not only with Judd.

Calling Skylar was more difficult. She was the wild, defiant one, and was not going to take this news well. When Sky came to visit their father in his last days, it had been four years since Cait had seen her. Skylar had her own life, living in Lexington, Kentucky, with her mother, but had a stake here, too.

Without another thought, Cait made the call. Usually she had to leave a message on voice mail, but today her sister answered.

"Hi, Sky. It's Caitlyn."

"What's wrong? You only phone when something's wrong."

As with Maddie, she told her the truth, not sugarcoating any of it.

"You're kidding me."

"No. The cash flow has stopped and the ranch is in dire straits."

"Why, Caitlyn? Why isn't High Five making a profit? It's a big ranch with a lot of cattle, and it's always been profitable. What's the problem?"

Skylar was pointing the finger straight at her. How dare she! "Maybe if you came home more often, you'd know."

"Maybe if you were a better manager we wouldn't be in this fix."

"If you think you can do a better job, then get your ass here and try."

"Don't get huffy with me. If you'd just married the damn man, we wouldn't be in this mess."

"Excuse me?" Both of their tempers had flown the coop, so to speak, and Caitlyn wasn't backing down or admitting fault. This was typical of their relationship, with the two of them always at loggerheads.

"You know what I mean."

"My relationship with Judd or lack thereof has nothing to do with this. Dad sold our oil and gas royalties and now we have to decide what we're going to do. You need to come home."

"There is no way I can just drop everything and leave at a moment's notice."

"That's up to you. Maddie and I will make decisions without you."

"Like hell." There was a momentary pause. "Listen, Cait. I need that money."

"I heard the same thing from Maddie. And I might remind you that I put my money back into High Five. You two have been living free and easy. That's going to stop. I'm sorry, but it is. If you want to change things, then come home. That's my last word."

"Cait—"

"No, Sky. I'm not listening to any more of your mouth. If you think you can run this ranch better, you're welcome to try. *Just get here!*" She shouted the last words into the receiver and slammed it down.

Caitlyn stood and paced, trying to release her pent-up emotions. Sky didn't know how bad their father's drinking and gambling habits had been, nor did she know about Gran's fragile state of mind. Neither did Maddie.

Cait had shouldered the burden, while her sisters had lived a life of luxury. She ran her hands over her face with a deep, torturous sigh. She should have told them. Was this her fault?

Dropping her hands, she glanced out the window toward the Southern Cross. *I'll take everything you love.* Judd's words took root in her thoughts, her emotions. Yes, it was her fault. All because she wouldn't marry a man who didn't love her.

At nineteen, she'd believed in love and happily ever after. She'd thought she'd hit the jackpot, only to discover that the marriage had been arranged between Jack Calhoun and her father. That's why Judd had shown an interest in her, after ignoring her for years.

It was all planned. Caitlyn was to do as she was told. But her father didn't count on her stubborn streak.

She'd wanted to marry for love, and wouldn't settle for less.

Now, years later, she had to wonder if love was real or just a fantasy that lived inside foolish women's hearts and minds.

For her, it was something she'd never experience again.

Love had died.

Only revenge remained.

CHAPTER FOUR

"CAITLYN, WHERE ARE YOU? I can't traipse all over the house looking for you. I'm too old for this. You have a visitor, so get your butt out here."

Etta's annoyed voice snapped Caitlyn out of her malaise. She hurried to the door and yanked it open, finding the housekeeper there with a wooden spoon in her hand.

As a kid, Cait had often felt the sting of that spoon on her legs, mostly for doing something she'd been told not to. She had a feeling Etta wanted to swat her with it now.

"What is it?"

"You have a visitor. He's in the parlor."

"He, who?"

"Mr. Calhoun."

Oh great, just what she needed. Two encounters with the man in one day. What did he want now? Her blood?

Etta leaned in and whispered, "What's he doing here?" Those faded brown eyes demanded an answer. Gran's faculties might be faulty, but Etta's were not. Cait knew she couldn't slip anything past her.

"I'm not sure. I'll go see."

Etta's bony fingers wrapped around her forearm, stopping her. "Don't lie to me, girl."

"High Five's in trouble. I'll explain later."

"Fine." She released her hold. "Did you check on Miss Dorie?"

"Yes. She's digging clothes out of the trunk and reliving happier times."

"Lordy, Lordy, is she ever gonna snap out of it?"

"We just have to be patient and gentle with her."

"Yeah." Etta glanced toward the parlor. "What are you waiting for?"

Cait smiled briefly. "Maybe a shot of courage."

Etta held up the spoon. "Will this help?"

"You bet."

Moments later, Caitlyn walked into the room, her boots dragging on the hardwood floor. The parlor looked the same as it had in the seventies, with velvet drapes and heavy antique furniture. Judd stood in the middle of the room on an Oriental rug that had seen better days. He held his hat in his hand, along with more blasted papers.

Oh, yes, a gentleman always removed his hat in the company of a lady. Judd had always had impeccable manners. Too bad they didn't come with real emotion, real feelings.

"What is it, Judd?" She stood a good twelve feet away, but still felt the power of his presence. Her lungs squeezed tight and a feeling from her past surfaced. She was nineteen, young and in—oops... The four-letter word wasn't in her vocabulary anymore. She'd replaced it with one that would scorch his ears.

"You left in such a hurry you forgot your copy of the sale of the royalties and your father's codicil to his will. You might need them to show your sisters." Judd held the papers toward her.

She crossed her arms and made no move to take them. "You could have sent someone with them. Brenda Sue goes right by here on her way home. Why are *you* here?"

Her direct question didn't faze him. He laid the papers on an end table by the settee. Cait noticed the film of dust there. Damn! Etta's eyes weren't the best anymore and Cait didn't have time for housework. She had a ranch to run. And what did she care if Judd saw their home wasn't immaculate.

"I had a reason for coming," he said, jolting her out of her thoughts.

"What would that be?"

His eyes caught and held hers. She wanted to

look away but couldn't. "I wanted to urge you once again to sell now and get it over with."

She cocked an eyebrow. "You don't think I can run this ranch successfully without the royalties?"

"You haven't so far."

"I—"

He held up a hand. "Don't make this about you and me. Do what's right for your family."

"*You* made this about you and me." Her voice rose with anger. "You want me to pay for daring to walk away from Judd Calhoun. Maybe even beg. It ain't happening, mister."

His lips formed a thin line. "I was harsh this afternoon. A lot of that old resentment came back. Bottom line, Caitlyn, you lived away from here a lot of years. It shouldn't be a problem to do that again."

"I lived away because my father didn't want me here. It wasn't voluntary." Despite every effort, she couldn't keep the hurt out of her voice.

"You made that decision. No one else."

She stepped closer to him, his woodsy masculine scent doing a number on her senses. "Yes, I did. At the time, you didn't even care enough to ask why I made that decision."

He gripped his Stetson so tight he bent the rim. "You wanted me to beg you to stay?"

"No. I wanted to talk. I wanted to have a say in our wedding, our marriage, our life."

He drew back. "I don't know what the hell you're talking about. You planned the wedding."

"Oh, please." She rolled her eyes. "I was to wear your mother's wedding dress and the wedding would be at Southern Cross. Soon after, I was to produce babies and heirs, preferably all male."

He frowned deeply. "My father requested that you wear my mother's dress and—"

"No. He demanded, and you backed him up." She cut him off faster than a road hog on the freeway. "I was never asked. Every freaking woman on the planet dreams of picking out her own damn wedding dress."

"It's a little late to be discussing this now."

"You got it, so take your offer of a sale and stuff it. I have six months and I'm taking every second of that time."

"Your sisters might have something to say about that."

"I can handle my sisters."

He stared at her and she resisted the urge to move away. He was too close, too powerful. But she stood her ground, despite shaky knees and an even shakier disposition.

"You've gotten hard, Caitlyn," he remarked, his eyes roaming over her face. Heat rose in her abdomen and traveled up to bathe her cheeks.

"Really? Your own edges are so hard they'd cut glass," she retorted.

His eyes met hers then. "That's what you did to us." Saying that, he walked out.

She sucked in a breath and an errant tear slipped from her eye. He had to have the last word, and it was effective, engaging all her feminine emotions. Guilt invaded her conscience and that made her mad.

Judd Calhoun would not get to her.

AFTER SUPPER, they sat at the kitchen table and talked about the future. Etta, Rufus and Cooper were all the help Caitlyn had, and they always ate together. Cooper lived in the bunkhouse, and Etta and Rufus's home was the first log cabin that Caitlyn's forefathers had built on the property.

Etta took a seat after checking on Gran. Cait had decided not to tell her grandmother until she felt Gran was ready to hear the news.

"How is she?" Cait asked.

"Still playing with those old clothes. Miss Dorie needs to get a grip on reality, but I don't know how she's going to handle what's happening now. Lordy, Lordy." Etta shook her head. "But I know one thing. I'm not playing Prissy from *Gone with the Wind* again. Enough is enough."

"Now you'd make a good Prissy," Ru said,

chewing on a toothpick. "A mite too skinny, though."

"Now you listen here—"

Caitlyn made a time-out sign. "Take a breather. We have bigger problems than Gran's make-believe. I'm open for suggestions."

Coop rested his forearms on the old oak table. "June is a couple of days away and we'll have plenty of hay to bale. We can keep what we need and sell the rest. And, of course, sell some of the stock."

Cait took a sip of her tea. "I only want to do that as a last resort. Without cattle we can't operate this ranch."

"Don't worry about my wages, Cait," Coop said. "I have a place to live, and food. All I need are a few bucks for beer, and gas for my truck."

"Same goes for Etta and me," Rufus added.

"I appreciate everyone's help. My sisters will be here in a few days and we'll decide what to do."

"No offense—" Coop swiped a hand through his sandy-blond hair "—but they're city girls. They don't know much about ranching."

"They're owners of High Five, though, same as me."

"Yep." Ru reached for his worn hat. "Things are getting rough around here. I think I'll mosey over to our place and stretch out for a while."

"Just wipe your feet before you go in," Etta told him.

"Woman, don't be a pain in my ass."

Cait was in the process of interrupting when there was a loud knock on the back door.

Chance Hardin, Etta and Rufus's nephew, poked his head in. "Hey, I wondered where everyone was."

When Etta's brother and sister-in-law were killed in a car accident, Etta and Rufus had taken in their three boys. Chance was the only one still around High Cotton, and he checked on his aunt and uncle often.

"Chance." Etta threw herself at him and hugged him tightly.

"Let him go, for heaven sakes," Ru said. "You're gonna choke him to death."

Cait noticed Ru squeezing Chance's shoulder, too. They were both glad to see him.

Etta drew back, her bony fingers smoothing her nephew's chambray shirt. "Why didn't you call and let us know you were coming? We'd have waited supper. Are you hungry? We have plenty."

"No. I've already eaten. I was just passing by and wanted to say hi."

"Hi, Chance," Caitlyn said.

"Ah, Cait, the most beautiful woman in High Cotton."

She grinned. "Yeah. Me and every woman you meet."

He met her grin with a stellar one of his own. "Damn. Beautiful and smart. Can't beat that with a sledgehammer." He turned to Cooper. "Hey, Coop."

"Chance." The cowboy shook his hand. "What are you doing these days?"

"Working my butt off for the big oil companies."

"You still out on the rigs?"

"You bet. Pays good money. We're drilling over at the McGruder place, about thirty miles from here."

"I know. I've been by the place a few times and saw a lot dump trucks going in and out of there."

"Yeah. Old man McGruder is smart as a whip. This is the second well we've drilled on his property, and he probably has money coming out the wazoo. But now he's selling sand and gravel off his land."

"Who buys it, and for what?" Cait asked curiously.

"He sold a lot of sand and gravel to the oil company. They have to have it to build roads to the oil pads, so the big rig and trucks can go in and out without getting stuck. Of course, we had to have water for drilling, so Mr. McGruder got a new water well. They use the pea gravel for drilling, too. He's also selling sand to a home builder who uses it for the foundation of new houses."

"Bart did that back in the eighties when things got a little tight," Rufus said.

"Where?" Cait asked, not remembering that.

"The southwest pasture. We don't run cattle there."

"How about some pie?" Etta interrupted.

Caitlyn picked up the leftover chocolate pie from the table and handed it to her. "Go spend some time with Chance. I'll clean the kitchen."

"No, I—"

Cait gently nudged them out the door, knowing they wanted to visit.

"I'll help," Coop offered.

Within minutes they had the kitchen clean. Cait laid the dish towel over the edge of the sink.

"Are you okay?" the cowboy asked.

She wiped her hands down her faded jeans. "Not really. I don't know how I'm going to save this ranch. With the oil and gas royalties, I was able to rebuild the herd Dad had sold. We were just getting to a point were we might show a profit. But if we have to sell off cows that won't happen."

"A calf crop will be ready to market in June. That will help."

"Yeah, but it won't be enough to see us through a dry summer." She massaged her temples. "It's a bitch when the past comes back and bites you in the butt."

Coop leaned against the cabinet. "How much gambling money did your dad owe?"

Cait dropped her hands. "I didn't ask." And she should have. Where was her brain? Going down guilt avenue at full throttle. Damn it. That should have been her first question. But her senses were too busy remembering what it was like to be in love with Judd.

"Those people are not pleasant when they don't get their money."

"Judd mentioned that."

"Maybe Judd was the only solution for Dane, for High Five."

She pointed a finger at Cooper. "Oh, please. Don't you dare go over to his side."

"I'm not, but you know how your father was. He never had a spending limit."

"I know." She stretched her shoulders, wishing she could close her eyes and the nightmare would go away.

"I saw Judd's truck here this afternoon."

"Yeah. He was doing what he does best, pressuring me to sell."

There was silence for a moment.

"I wasn't here all those years ago when you broke the engagement, but I assume you had a good reason."

Cait thought about that. Would a man understand? Cooper was her best friend. She told him a lot of things, but sharing her feelings about Judd wasn't on the table.

"Okay, that's a little personal, and I don't do personal," Coop said quickly. "Think I'll head to the bunkhouse and nurse a beer."

"Think I'll head to the study and nurse a gigantic headache named Judd Calhoun."

Coop smiled. "See you in the morning."

Caitlyn walked upstairs to check on Gran. She was curled up on a chaise longue, asleep in a dress from the forties, with her long white hair cascading over her shoulder.

Kissing her wrinkled cheek, Cait whispered, "Dream on, Gran." With a sigh, she sank down to the floor beside her. Resting her head on her grandmother's hand, she picked up a high-necked dress from the thirties.

So many people depended on her: Gran, her sisters, Etta, Rufus and Cooper. What would they do if High Five was sold?

Judd had her by… What was it that guys said? By the short hairs? All she knew was that Judd had her where it hurt. Bad.

She fingered the dress, which smelled of mothballs, willing herself to come up with a way to get the money she needed to save her home.

Wait a minute. She sat up straight and threw the dress into the trunk. Why hadn't she thought of it before?

CHAPTER FIVE

EARLY THE NEXT MORNING Caitlyn was on the way to Mr. McGruder's. She wanted information about selling sand and gravel. She could have called, but Mr. McGruder was the kind of man who responded better when talking face-to-face. Being of the older generation, he didn't care for phones all that much. He liked the personal touch.

It didn't take her long to get the buyer's name and number. She didn't ask about price because she knew McGruder wouldn't divulge it.

Back in her office, she called only to learn the man had all the suppliers he needed. Damn! She told him to keep her in mind if he ever needed another one, and gave him her name and phone number.

By the time she hung up, all the excitement had oozed out of her and she felt stupid. Their financial situation wasn't going to be that easy to fix. There must be a black cloud over her head or something, but she didn't have time to wallow in misery. There was work to be done.

She saddled Jazzy, her brown quarter horse, and set out to join Coop and Rufus. Red neighed from across the fence. The mare didn't like it when Cait rode another horse, but Jaz was for work. Red she rode for pleasure.

The day was already getting hot. Cait pulled her straw hat lower to shade her face. Her arms were protected from the sun by a long-sleeved, pearl-snap shirt. The sun was hell on a woman's skin.

Coop came to meet her riding a bay gelding. "We have a good count of calves in this pasture to go in June, and we have a lot more on the ground, maybe a September sale."

They ran a mixed-breed cow-and-calf operation now. Cait's father had sold the registered stock years ago. In High Five's heyday her great-grandfather would have nothing but pure-breds on his property. But it took time and money to keep records of an animal's ancestry, so that wasn't an option for the ranch anymore.

"We can make this work." Coop glanced around at the knee-deep coastal the cows and calves were standing in. "They have plenty to eat and all we have to do is supply water, salt and minerals."

Cait moved restlessly in the saddle. "It's the summer I'm worried about. When the coastal has been eaten and we have barren dry ground."

"We'll rotate the pastures like always."

Cait's gaze swept over the grazing cattle. "Where's Ru?"

"Checking the windmill."

"Good. We have to make sure they have water at all times."

"I'm heading for the northeast pasture. Catch you later." Coop kneed his horse and then pulled up again. "Whoa, we got company."

Cait noticed the riders, too—Albert Harland, the Southern Cross foreman, and two cowboys. Harland was mean as a rattlesnake, sneaky as a ferret, and resembled the latter. His number one goal was to make life as miserable as possible for Caitlyn. He thought she was uppity and didn't know her place.

He stopped just short of galloping into her. If he thought she was going to show fear, then the man didn't have a brain cell that was actively working.

"Mornin', Miss Belle." He tipped his hat and grinned like a possum eating persimmons.

"Harland." She folded her hands over the saddle horn. "Is there a problem?"

"Yep." The saddle protested from his weight. "The fence is down again on this pasture. One of your bulls, the big black one, keeps getting into our registered cows, and Mr. Calhoun would appreciate it if you'd take care of your fences and keep your mangy bull away. It costs us money every time he breeds a cow. You got it?"

Anger shot through her veins like a rocket. "I got it."

"And if I catch that bull on the Southern Cross again, I'll shoot him. Do I make myself clear?"

"You bag of—"

Harland broke into Coop's effusive tirade. "Yates, if I catch you on the Southern Cross, I'll shoot first and ask questions later. Ex-cons aren't welcome there." He jerked his reins to turn his horse, but Caitlyn reached out and grabbed them, effectively stopping the horse. And rider.

"What the hell?" the foreman spluttered.

"Let's get one thing straight, Harland. That gun business works both ways. If Judd Calhoun doesn't want to see a lot of dead registered cows sprawled on his property, then I suggest you think twice before shooting my bull."

"Why, you—"

"And if you even look crossways at Cooper, you're gonna have a whole lot of mad woman coming your way. Got it?"

"Bitch," Harland muttered, and jerked his horse away.

"Give your boss the message," she shouted as they rode off her land.

"Damn, Cait." Coop stared at her with a startled expression. "You can bullshit better than anyone I know." His eyes narrowed. "Or did you mean that?"

She shifted uncomfortably in the saddle. "Actually, if I had to shoot any living thing, I'd probably throw up." She lifted an eyebrow. "But I can talk a good game. I did mean what I said about you, though." She turned her horse. "Now let's go get ol' Boss before he gets us into any more trouble."

They'd named the bull Boss because he fought every bull that came within his chosen territory. He liked having the cream of the crop, and usually that included their neighbor's cows.

Caitlyn and Cooper crossed onto Judd's ranch through the broken barbed wire, and found the bull easily, smack-dab in the middle of a herd of high-class registered cows. He was busy sniffing every animal in sight.

"This could prove to be a little difficult," Coop said, pulling up alongside Cait. The two of them watched the two-thousand-pound bull chasing cows. "He's not going to like having his fun interrupted."

"Any ideas?" she asked as she caught sight of Harland and his cowboys on the horizon. They were watching, waiting for her to make a fool of herself.

"The old-fashioned way?" Coop suggested.

"Okay." She knew cattle and she knew horses, and both were unpredictable. Cait wasn't counting on Boss being docile and following her to High Five. He was in the midst of sealing a thirty-second love affair with a high-priced cow, and he wasn't going to take their intrusion kindly. "Let's give our quarter horses a workout. Ready?"

"Yep. Watch those sawed-off horns."

"I'll take the left," Cait said as she meandered into the herd. Coop moved to the right of the bull.

The cows scattered, and as soon as Boss spotted the riders, he swung his head in an agitated manner and pawed at the ground with a you'll-never-take-me stance. Cait patted Jaz's neck. "Okay, let's show him who's the boss."

They effectively cut him away from the herd, and Boss wasn't happy. He charged, but Jaz did her magic, swinging back and forth, not letting him get by. The bull charged the other way, but Coop was there, blocking his path. Boss swung toward Cait again and she let Jaz work the way she'd been trained. The quick moves had Cait on full alert. She had to stay focused and not lose her balance.

As the bull switched gears and charged toward Coop yet again, Caitlyn pulled the Hot-Shot cattle prod from her saddle and rode in and zapped the animal from the rear.

Not liking the sting, Boss spun round and round, snot flying from his nose, and then made a dead run for High Five.

"Hot damn," Coop shouted. He rode right on the bull's tail, whooping and hollering.

Jaz was ready to run, too, and Cait had a hard time controlling her. As Jaz pranced around, Cait saw that Judd had joined Harland and the boys. There was no mistaking him. She backed up Jaz with a quick step, thumbed her nose at the watching crowd, then hightailed it for High Five. She didn't even mind eating Coop's and Boss's dust.

"Yee haw," she cried, just for the hell of it, immensely grateful she hadn't made a fool of herself. Or maybe that was a matter of opinion.

When she caught up with Coop, he was watching Boss refamiliarize himself with the High Five herd, sniffing each cow to make sure he hadn't missed one while he was rambling.

"That bull has one insatiable appetite."

"It keeps calves on the ground," Cait said, trying not to smile. "Now let's fix that fence." She turned Jaz and saw the rider coming their way. "Now what?"

Judd, tall and impressive in the saddle, was headed toward her. He rode a magnificent black stallion, as magnificent as the man himself. Both exuded strength, power and a touch of splendor. And she could be suffering from too much sun, because Judd had more of a touch of the devil than of splendor.

"I'm going to get Rufus," Coop said. "You're on your own."

"Gee, thanks." She nudged her horse forward to meet her neighbor, wiping dust from her mouth with the back of her hand. At that moment she realized what a sight she must look, with dust from her hat to her boots and sweat staining her blouse. She smelled as foul as her horse, and the fact rubbed like a cocklebur against the feminine side of her nature.

"Why are you playing rodeo in my herd?"

"I was told to get my bull out, and that's what I did." She kept her voice neutral and didn't react to his angry tone.

"My boys could have cut him out much easier." His tone didn't change.

She rose a bit in the saddle and the leather creaked. "I thought I did a damn good job myself, considering time was of the essence."

He squinted against the noonday sun. "What do you mean?"

"Harland said he was going to shoot him if I didn't get him out in a nanosecond. Something about 'registered cows' and 'Judd Calhoun wasn't pleased.'"

His face tightened into those taut lines she knew so well. "I never said anything about shooting the bull. You have my word he won't be shot. Just keep the damn animal on your property."

A quick thank-you rose in her throat, but his last sentence killed the idea like a blast from a shotgun, successfully scattering it to the saner regions of her mind.

"That's what I'm doing," she said through clenched teeth.

He motioned over his shoulder. "I'll have the fence repaired."

"I can fix the fence."

"I want it done right and not half-ass."

Any other time she would have spat holy hell at his high-handedness. But it would take money to repair the fence properly, money she didn't have. For the sake of High Five she pushed her pride aside. And the weight was heavy. It took her a full minute to nod her head.

He stood in the stirrups and picked up his reins. Suddenly he eased his butt back against the leather, his black eyes holding hers with a gleam she remembered from her younger days—a gleam of playful teasing. Talk about a blast from the past. It was so unexpected it almost knocked her out of the saddle.

"Your blouse is open."

She glanced down and saw that two snaps were undone, revealing the white lace of her bra. They must have come open when she was bulldogging Boss. *Oh, sh…*

Raising her eyes to his, she replied, "I know. I like it that way. It's cooler."

"It might give Yates the wrong idea."

"Maybe. But that's none of your business."

He inclined his head, and she wondered if he remembered all the times he had undone her blouse, and what had followed afterward. With all the women who'd followed her in his life, she doubted it. But she remembered the tantalizing brush of his fingers and the excitement that had leaped through her—much as it was doing now. Some memories were gold plated and stored in secret places. Why she'd chosen this moment to review them was unclear.

"Enjoy the fresh air." He kneed the stallion, and the horse responded beautifully, turning on a dime and kicking up dirt. She watched rider and horse until they disappeared into the distance.

Then she slowly snapped her shirt closed.

JUDD GAVE BARON HIS HEAD and they flew through fields of coastal and herds of cattle. They sliced through the wind effortlessly, but no matter how fast the stallion ran, Judd couldn't outrun the fire in his gut from when he'd looked at Caitlyn.

He shouldn't feel this way after all these years. How could he hate her and react like this? All he could think about was reaching out and undoing the rest of those snaps, lifting her from the saddle and then sliding with her to the grass. Nothing existed but the two of them, and together they rode to places only lovers knew about....

His hat flew off and he slowed. He turned Baron and headed back for it. Reaching down, he swiped it from the ground. After dusting it off, he galloped toward home. And put every memory of Caitlyn out of his mind. That came easy. He'd been doing it for years.

Over the ridge, Harland and the cowboys were waiting. Judd stopped.

"Get supplies and fix that fence today," he said to the foreman. "I don't want that bull back in my herd."

"You want us to fix the fence?" Harland asked, a touch of sarcasm in his voice.

Being second-guessed rubbed Judd the wrong way. Harland questioned too many of his orders, and he wanted it stopped.

"Do you have a problem with that?" he asked, his eyes locking with the other man's.

"No, sir, but—"

"On the Southern Cross, I'm the boss and what I say goes. If that doesn't suit you, you're welcome to leave. Now."

"C'mon, Judd, I've worked here a long time. I

just thought Miss Belle should be the one to fix the fence. Her bull broke it."

"Miss Belle would only patch it. I want it fixed right. In a few months her place will become a part of Southern Cross and I don't want to have to redo it."

Harland grinned. "I knew you had a damn good reason. I'll get the boys right on it."

"Another thing, and I hope I'm clear about this—do not shoot that bull or any neighbor's animal that strays onto our property. I don't do business that way. Am I clear?"

"Yes, sir. I was only trying to scare her."

"Miss Belle doesn't scare that easily."

Judd kneed Baron and rode on toward the barn. Nothing scared Caitlyn, except losing High Five. That was her deepest fear and he knew it. Knowing your enemy's weakness was half the battle. Victory was just a matter of time.

It was his goal, what he'd dreamed about for fourteen years. But as he dismounted, all he could see and think about was her open blouse and the curve of her breast.

CHAPTER SIX

CAITLYN RODE BACK TO THE house about two to check on Gran. She hadn't been up when Cait had left that morning.

Chance's truck was parked outside, and when she went in, Gran, Etta and he were at the table, just finishing lunch. Gran was dressed in her normal slacks and blouse, and her hair was pinned at her nape. She looked like she used to, and Cait prayed her grandmother was back to her old self.

"Caitlyn, baby, we have a visitor," Gran said. "Chance is having lunch with us."

He winked. "Etta wouldn't let me leave without eating one of her home-cooked meals."

"We see you so little." Etta carried dishes to the sink.

Caitlyn placed her hat on the rack. "Leaving so soon?"

"Yep." Chance stood. "We're through at the McGruders and we're packing up and heading for east Texas." He kissed his aunt's cheek. "I'll call. Thanks for the lunch, Miss Dorie."

Caitlyn followed him outside. "Would you do me a favor, please?"

Chance settled his hat on his head. "Anything, beautiful lady."

"If you hear of anyone needing sand or gravel, would you send them my way?"

"Sure. Etta told me about High Five's problem. I'm sorry, Cait."

"Thank you. Find me a buyer and I'll love you forever."

"Yeah." He smiled broadly. "They all say that."

She waved as he drove away, and then she went back inside.

Gran was on the phone. Replacing the receiver, she smiled at Caitlyn. "That was Madison. She's coming for a visit." Dorie looked past Cait. "Is your father with you? He's going to be so excited."

Cait felt as if someone had just lassoed her around the neck and yanked the rope tight. She struggled to breathe. Gran was not back to normal. The doctors had said to tell her the truth, so that's what Cait did, even though it made her throat feel rusty and dry.

"Gran, Dad is dead."

"Yes." A look of sadness clouded her brown eyes. "I forget sometimes."

Caitlyn hugged her. "It's okay to forget—sometimes."

But Cait never forgot, not for a second. Her father's death filled her every waking moment and all the dreams that tortured her nights. She wasn't the son he'd wanted. At her age she should be beyond that childhood feeling of inadequacy. Why wasn't she?

Gran drew back, her eyes bright with unshed tears. "But it's exciting that Maddie's coming home, isn't it?"

"Yes, it is. When is she arriving?"

Gran frowned. "I forget."

"Don't worry about it," Cait reassured her. She would call Maddie back.

"Okay. I'm going upstairs, to pull out all the dresses that will look great on Madison. With her blond hair and blue eyes, she'd make a great Ingrid Bergman. *Casablanca*. Oh, yes, we're going to have so much fun."

Cait sighed and scrubbed her face with her hands. She wanted her grandmother back—the one who didn't live in a make-believe world.

Etta patted her shoulder. "Dorie will be fine. She's just grieving."

"I don't know. It's been over two months now."

"Stop worrying. You have to get a move on. Maddie's plane lands in Austin at four."

Cait whirled around. "What?"

"I answered the phone and that's what she said."

"Good grief, I could use a little notice. It's not like I'm sitting here cleaning the dirt from under my nails."

"Well, I'm sure they could use it." Etta reached for the plate of leftover fried chicken.

Caitlyn looked at her nails. Holy moly. They were broken off short and caked with dirt. How unattractive was that? They were a worker's hands. She'd almost forgotten how to feel feminine.

She touched the collar of her shirt. No, she hadn't forgotten. She'd felt it today when Judd had stared at her breasts.

She threw that emotion into the trash bin of her thoughts. That's where it needed to stay. And that's where Judd Calhoun would stay, too.

A few minutes later, Caitlyn was driving Gran's old Lincoln, munching on a chicken leg and heading for Austin, almost two hours away. She'd taken the sedan because she was afraid her truck wouldn't make it. Turning up the radio, she leaned back and enjoyed the ride.

The traffic wasn't bad on U.S. 290 or Texas 21. As she neared Bastrop Highway it became a little congested, as it was on Presidential Boulevard in Austin, leading to the terminal.

Glancing at her watch, she saw it was already

after four. By the time she reached the baggage and pickup area she was definitely late.

With her blond hair, her sister was easy to spot. Maddie placed her case on the backseat and slipped into the passenger side. She wore gray slacks and a powder-blue top, with her hair in a neat bob around her face.

"Hey, big sis." Madison hugged and kissed her, then wrinkled her nose. "Whatever perfume you're using, it's not working."

"Very funny. I was on the range and didn't get your message until almost two. I didn't have time to change, so don't give me any lip."

A car honked behind them.

"Keep your britches on," Cait said into her rearview mirror, and drove off.

"We can't go far," Maddie told her.

"Why not?"

"I got a call from Sky, and her plane is coming in at five."

"It would be nice if the two of you would call me and let me know these things."

"I tried three times this morning and no one answered, so don't give *me* any lip." Maddie held up a hand for a high five, something they'd done since they were kids.

They slapped hands. "I was out early, Gran

was asleep and Chance was at Etta's, so I guess she was late."

"Sky tried, too, and couldn't get anyone. That's why she called me."

Cait maneuvered through the traffic. "I'll have to go out and circle back."

"Sky should be there by then."

Cait's full attention was on the traffic zooming by the old Lincoln, and nothing else was said.

"How's Gran?" Maddie finally asked, keeping an eye on the traffic, too.

"Not good. She hasn't adjusted to Dad's death. She even forgets he is dead. Most of the time she plays make-believe with those old clothes she's saved from her Broadway days."

"I love playing make-believe with Gran. It's a special memory of my childhood."

"Mine, too, but it's different now." Cait made the turn onto Presidential Boulevard. "You'll see when you get home."

"It won't be the same without Dad there," Maddie said, her voice laced with sadness.

"I know. I—"

"There's Skylar." Maddie pointed to the striking redhead with the impatient expression, standing at the curb.

Cait knew it was Sky, but it didn't look like her flashy sister. Her hair was clipped back and she wore black slacks, a white blouse and no-nonsense shoes. No jewelry. Very little makeup. She could pass for a nun. This couldn't be her sister—the one whose best friend was a mirror.

Cait pulled up and Skylar slid into the backseat. "Where in the hell have you been? I've been standing out here for ten minutes."

Oh, yeah. Now *this* was her sister.

"I'm sorry, your highness. I'm a little late with my pick-up schedule."

"Shut up, Cait."

"*You* shut up," she retorted.

Suddenly all three burst out laughing. Sky leaned over the seat and patted Cait's and Maddie's shoulders. "It's so good to see both of you. Sorry I'm so bitchy. I think I have permanent PMS."

"You've been that way since you were about five, so I don't think you can blame it on that." Cait snickered.

"Don't start with me!" Skylar warned. Without a pause, she added, "How's Gran?"

Cait told her what she'd told Maddie.

"Gran has always loved to play make-believe. That's nothing new." Sky looked behind them. "I think you just ran a red light."

"I did not. It was yellow."

"And you're always right."

Cait glanced at her in the rearview mirror.

"Remember that when we discuss the ranch, which we'll do at home and not in the car."

"You're bossy, but you've always been that way."

"We have bitchy and bossy, so what am I?" Maddie asked.

"Hmm." Cait thought about it. "How about Betty Crocker sweet?"

"Oh, please." Maddie sighed. "I can be bitchy and bossy."

Both her sisters guffawed at that and then Sky leaned over the seat. "I don't think the ranch is in as bad a shape as you say, and I think Gran is fine, too. You're exaggerating."

Cait gritted her teeth and changed the subject. The rest of the way home they talked about their childhood. Maddie and Sky would have to see the ranch for themselves. It wasn't the showplace it once was. Sky had only stayed for a little while when their father had passed. Maddie knew more of the situation, but didn't offer any comments.

They reached Giddings and turned onto a county road that led to High Cotton. The place was barely a stop in the road—a convenience store–gas station combo; a general store that sold feed and hardware; a post office, community center, water and utilities building; two beer joints, one on each side of the road.

Caitlyn pulled into the gas station. "I better fill up

before we go home. Gran gets really mad if the tank is empty."

They all climbed out. Cait undid the gas cap and inserted the nozzle just as Brenda Sue drove up in her Corolla.

"Hi, there, Caitlyn," the blonde gushed as she got out. "I have to get my kids snacks. You know how kids are—always wanting something." Her gaze swung to her passengers. "You don't have to tell me. I know these are your sisters. I met y'all years ago at a Fourth of July barbecue on High Five. Your dad sure knew how to throw a party, and he was showing off his girls. You probably don't remember me because I didn't stay around long. I had a big crush on Chance Hardin and I was more interested in seeing him. You know how that is. I'll catch y'all later."

Sky and Maddie stared after her. "What the hell was that?" Sky asked. "My head is buzzing."

"A girl I went to school with. She has a hard time taking a breath." Cait grinned.

"Talk about a run-on sentence," Maddie declared.

Sky looked around. "How do you live in this hick place?"

"It's home. It's all I know and it's everything I love."

Sky and Maddie exchanged glances.

"I'll pay for the gas and we'll be on our way to

see Gran." Walking away, she felt the dent in her heart and in her pride. Her sisters had never viewed High Five the way she had, and she knew she had a big fight coming.

CAIT DROVE DOWN the dirt road to High Five, dust billowing behind them. The garages Grandpa Bart had built were in back. A covered walkway connected them to the house. He'd put in the garage for his beloved Dorie, so she could have easy access in inclement weather.

Pulling into Gran's spot, Cait slid the gearshift into Park and got out. Madison and Skylar followed.

Sky looked toward the barn. "When I was here for Dad's funeral, I did notice things were in disrepair. Maybe you didn't exaggerate that part."

"I haven't exaggerated anything."

At that moment, Coop and Rufus rode in from a day's work on the range.

Sky watched Cooper closely. "Why you hired an ex-con is beyond me. Have you thought he might be stealing from you? Maybe that's the reason we're in such a mess."

"Cooper is a fine, honest, hardworking man, and I trust him. If you want to keep all that red hair on your head, then I suggest you button your bitchy mouth."

"And I suggest—"

"Stop it." Madison stomped her foot. "I'm not spending this visit refereeing you two. Grow up, for heaven sakes."

Caitlyn shrugged. "Betty Crocker has spoken."

They laughed, linked arms and made their way into the house. They'd always been like that—fighting like hellcats and in the next instant smiling and hugging. They were sisters and could make each other madder than anyone. And they loved one another just as fiercely. Cait hoped they could remember that in the days ahead.

CHAPTER SEVEN

A STOMACH-RUMBLING AROMA greeted them. Clearly, Etta had been preparing a special meal.

Madison hugged the older woman. "I could gain five pounds just by the smell in your kitchen."

"Lordy, Lordy." Etta smiled at them. "You girls are a sight for these sore old eyes. I made chicken and dressing with all the trimmings and I don't want to hear one word about any diets. Tonight we're celebrating."

"You won't get any complaints from me." Sky embraced Etta. "I love your cooking."

"Where's Gran?" Maddie asked.

"Upstairs trying on dresses, and I'm not running up those stairs one more time to see how a gown looks on her. My patience and bony legs only go so far."

"I'll check on her." Cait hurried through the dining room, then stopped so suddenly that Maddie and Sky bumped into her.

"Good heavens, Cait, you could at least..."

Sky's voice trailed off as they stared up at their grandmother on the staircase.

She wore a white muslin slip that had to be at least fifty years old. Her long white hair tumbled down her back and across her shoulders was draped… No, it couldn't be. But Cait glanced toward the parlor and saw that it most definitely *was*—the old hunter-green velvet curtain.

"'War, war, war.'" Gran placed the back of her hand against her forehead. "'I get so bored I could scream.'"

Oh, my God! Cait darted up the stairs. "Gran," she said softly.

The elderly woman looked at her, her eyes a little dazed. "Hi, baby. Scarlett O'Hara from *Gone with the Wind,* remember?"

Cait swallowed. "Yes, Gran. Let me take this." She removed the heavy drape. "Look who's here." Maddie and Sky came up the stairs.

Gran held out her arms. "Oh, my babies are home." Maddie and Sky hugged their grandmother, then Gran brushed away a tear. "Caitlyn, go get your father. He's going to be so happy."

The three sisters stood transfixed, almost paralyzed. Cait's throat felt raw and she didn't know if she could say those words again today. They hurt too much.

Maddie came to the rescue, sliding her arm

around Gran's waist. "Let's go upstairs so you can lie down."

"Okay."

Cait took Gran's free arm and they all walked her to her room. Sky threw back the comforter on the four-poster bed and Gran crawled in. Cait arranged the big pillows under her head the way she liked.

"Comfy?" she asked.

"Oh, yes. My girls are home." Gran closed her eyes, holding on to Maddie's and Sky's hands.

Cait left the room. She had to or she was going to burst into tears. It broke her heart to see their grandmother like this.

On the stairs, she picked up the drape where she'd left it, and carried it to the parlor. It smelled of dust and age.

The stool Gran had used to take down the curtain stood by the windows. She could have fallen, broken something. Suddenly everything was too much, and Cait sank to the floor, the velvet drape settling in a heap around her. She drew her knees up and rested her forehead on them. Tears she couldn't stop spilled from her eyes. She couldn't be this weak! But Gran was her soft spot, her Achilles' heel.

"Cait." Sky sat beside her. "You weren't exaggerating. I can't stand to see Gran like that."

She raised her head. "I can't either, and I don't know how to help her."

"Me neither, but I'll be here for a few days, so I can at least help out."

"That would be nice."

Maddie came into the room. "Gran's asleep. She's exhausted from trying on clothes." She picked up the velvet fabric. "Let's hang this."

Together they put the drape back in place. Maddie wiggled her nose. "It's very dusty."

"I don't have time for housework. That can be your job while you're here."

"Gee, thanks."

"Supper's ready," Etta called.

The sisters made their way into the kitchen, to find Rufus sitting at the table.

"Where's Cooper?" Cait asked.

The old cowboy shifted nervously in his chair. "He's at the bunkhouse. I'll take him a plate."

"Nonsense…"

"I'm glad he respects our privacy," Sky said. "I feel more comfortable that way."

Cait placed her hands on her hips. "I hope you never have to eat those words."

"Now, listen—"

"Sit down and stop this bickering," Etta added, and the two of them complied.

Supper was a subdued affair. They were thinking about Gran.

IN THE MORNING, Cait awoke early and went down to make coffee. She carried Gran a cup.

"Mornin', baby." Gran scooted up in bed. "It's always refreshing to see my sweet baby's face first thing in the day."

Cait handed her the coffee. "Gran, I'm hardly a baby."

"I know. You should be married." Her grandmother took a sip. "Have you seen Judd lately?"

The change of subject took her by surprise. She wanted Gran back to normal, but not where she could gauge her emotions and read her mind. Caitlyn fidgeted as she felt the old woman's eyes filleting her like a crappie, getting to the tasty part.

She gave her best I-couldn't-care-less impression. "In a town as small as High Cotton, it's hard to miss Judd Calhoun."

"Because he stands a head taller than the rest, and your heart goes pitter-patter every time you see him."

Cait kissed Gran's forehead, wanting to tell her what a snake in the grass Judd really was. But she could never hurt her. "Not exactly." It felt more like she'd been hit in the chest with a rock from a slingshot, and her heart reacted in spasms of pain and regret. "I have to go to work, and you have company."

Dorie's face scrunched into a frown—like the one she'd told Cait, as a child, never to make in case it caused wrinkles. That must be true, because Gran had very few wrinkles. On the other hand, Caitlyn could feel hers deepening daily.

"Company?" Gran sat up straight. "Oh, my, Madison and Skylar are here, aren't they? I remember now."

"Yes." Cait clenched her jaw and waited. *Please, please, don't ask me to go get my father.*

Gran handed Cait her cup and swung her feet over the side of the bed. "I have to see them."

The door swung open just then and Maddie and Sky rushed in, dressed in their sleeping attire, shorts and tanks tops. Not for the first time, Cait realized Maddie was way too thin.

Amid hugs, kisses and laughter, Caitlyn said, "I have to get Cooper and Rufus started for the day. I'll be back later."

"Cait?" Sky called.

She glanced back.

"We need to talk."

She nodded shortly, resenting that her sister felt she needed to remind her.

An hour later, Cait joined Skylar and Madison in the study. Her sisters sat across the desk, where she laid out the document their father had signed, selling High Five's oil and gas royalties. Sky whipped it up, quickly read through it and then shoved it at Maddie.

"It says you get to make the decision whether to sell or not. So what the hell are we doing here?" Anger laced Sky's accusing words.

"You're both part owners of High Five."

"But you can keep us in limbo for six months?"

"Yes. And I just might make a success of this ranch."

Sky laughed, a sound that ricocheted off Cait's nerve endings. "Keep dreaming and we're going to wind up with nothing. I can't believe Dad would do this to us."

Maddie placed the document on the desk. "I know how you feel about High Five, Cait, but... but I depend on my share of the money."

"I do, too," Sky added. "I'm barely getting by the way things are now. I'm sorry, but we need to sell."

Cait swallowed the retort that leaped to her throat. "What about Gran?"

Skylar crossed her legs and stared at a speck on her jeans. Maddie kept her eyes downward. Cait knew this wasn't easy for them. It wasn't easy for her, either.

She leaned forward, trying to make her point. "Every dime I've gotten from royalties has gone back into High Five. Dad pretty much left us penniless. Regardless, every month I mail you a check, and you're able to live a life of luxury. Not once have I asked for you to give any of it back. Now I'm asking for your understanding, for Gran and for me. High Five is her home, and I will fight tooth and nail to keep her here."

Sky looked straight at her. "We're not heartless. You're just fighting a losing battle. You're fighting Judd Calhoun."

"I'm aware of that."

"He's powerful and he'll squash you like a pesky roach. Heaven forbid that you would apologize and put an end to all this."

"What?" Cait went on red alert, a state she and Maddie had been familiar with when they were teenagers and Sky got in their faces. It was usually an all-out war when the stubborn, strong Belle sisters butted heads, as they were now.

"Tell Judd you're sorry, that you'll sleep with him, have his children, marry him and otherwise grovel at his feet every chance you get. You love High Five. That's what you have to do to make this problem go away. I know it. Maddie knows it. The whole damn world knows it. Why in the hell don't you?"

Cait leaped to her feet. "Shut up, Sky."

The redhead lifted an eyebrow. "You can't deny the truth. Judd's been waiting years for this opportunity, and Dad just handed it to him like a blank check. Could that be because Dad was still pissed at you for walking away from the best thing that could have happened to you? The best thing that could have happened to High Five? Now we're all paying for your mistakes. Your choices."

Cait wanted to jump across the desk and yank every red hair from Sky's head. But truth kept her rooted to the spot. Sometimes the evil monster was a hard foe to beat, and her sister wielded it better than anyone.

A whimpered, tortured sound left their other sister's throat. Cait was instantly at her side. "Maddie, what is it?"

She wiped away a tear. "I hate all this bickering. We can't go back and change the past. We have to deal with the now, the future."

Caitlyn knelt and leaned back on her heels. "There's something else, isn't there?" She knew that by Maddie's pale complexion and her trembling hands.

"I'm very emotional these days."

"Tell us why."

Madison wiped away another tear. "You remember about three years ago, when I got a job at a hospital as a counselor?"

"Yes." Cait caught Maddie's hands.

"Well, I had to have a physical. At the time I

was having a lot of cramping and excessive bleeding, so I had a complete checkup. Routine stuff, but…but the tumors on my ovaries weren't."

Cait's throat worked but no sound came out. Sky was also speechless.

"I had to have them removed, and then radiation and chemo. They said that, to save my life, I didn't have any options. Funny how they saved my life and took it away at the same time." She hiccupped. "I'll never be able to have a child."

"Oh, Maddie!" Cait hugged her, and Sky joined in. "I'm so sorry." She drew back. "That's why you're so thin and your hair is short."

"Yeah." Self-consciously, she lifted her hand to her head. "I'm growing a new batch."

"Why did you never tell us?" Cait asked.

"I just couldn't talk to anyone."

"Did Dad know?"

"I was getting chemo one day when he came for a visit, and my mom told him. I asked him not to tell anyone. I didn't want Gran or you all to worry."

"Are you okay now?"

Maddie shrugged. "As good as I'm going to get. I've been cancer free for two years, but I have enormous medical bills. That's why I need the money."

"Oh, Maddie. I'm sorry I was such a bitch." Cait hugged her again.

"I love High Five, but I have all these debts…."

Cait squeezed her hands. "Don't worry. We'll figure out something."

"I have a reason for needing the money, too," Sky said in a low voice.

"What reason?" Cait braced herself.

Sky got into a comfortable position, sitting cross-legged. "I need the money because I have… well, a child."

"Excuse me?"

"I have a child and…"

"You kept a child from us, your sisters and your grandmother?" Cait rose to her feet, feeling ticked off, really angry. "How could you do that?"

"It wasn't intentional. I was embarrassed, ashamed that I was so stupid. Todd told me repeatedly that he didn't want children. When he found out about the baby, he ended our affair and left. But his parents, who are wealthy, started calling and asking questions. I heard through a friend that they know about Kira and intend to gain custody. I can't let that happen, so I have to keep her hidden and a secret."

"Her name is Kira?" Maddie asked wistfully.

"Yes. She's three years old now, but from birth she cried all the time, and I had her in and out of the doctor's office for high fevers. I knew something was wrong, but the doc could never figure out what until her knee turned red and swollen. She has juvenile rheumatoid arthritis."

"Oh, no! I'm so sorry!" Cait's anger turned to sadness. "Did Dad know?"

Sky nodded. "Like with Maddie, he showed up one day unexpectedly, but he understood my reasons for secrecy. He wanted me to keep my child."

"Where is she now?" Maddie asked quietly.

"She's with my mother, which is why I can only stay a few days. I hope we'll be able to resolve this situation quickly. And for the record, I'm not enjoying a life of luxury. I live in a small apartment, and every dime goes toward my daughter's well-being."

Two pairs of eyes turned to Caitlyn. "Well, I think I have mud and egg on my face," she stated. "Anyone care to smack me?"

"Don't tempt me," Sky said with a grin, and then added, "Sometimes you're obsessed with High Five. Please look at this realistically, for all of us."

Cait sank to the floor again, unsure how to explain how she felt to her sisters.

When she remained silent, Maddie spoke up. "All those years ago, I know you loved Judd. I'd never seen you so happy. Gran and Renee were knee-deep in wedding plans, and Sky and I had been fitted for our dresses. Dad had five hundred people on the wedding list. It was going to be the biggest affair this small town had ever seen. What happened, Cait? You never told us what made you walk away."

She played with the French braid hanging over her shoulder, and suddenly the words came pouring out. "I was floating on a cloud back then. The most eligible, most handsome bachelor in the county had asked me to marry him. Suddenly I was the center of his world."

"That was good, right?" Sky asked.

Cait twisted the braid. "It would have been wonderful, except I heard Jack Calhoun and Dad talking. They had arranged the marriage, and Judd went along with it. It would be beneficial to both families."

Sky's mouth formed a big O.

"I could have lived with that, and all the plans being made without my input, even wearing Judd's mother's wedding dress. But there was one thing I couldn't live without."

"What?" Maddie voice was breathless.

"Judd's love."

"But he loved you," Sky pointed out. "He couldn't take his eyes off you."

"I thought so, too." Cait pulled the braid until her head hurt. "So I *asked* him if he loved me. Do you know what he said?"

"What? What?" Sky sounded like an excited child.

"He said we'd have a strong marriage and we'd be happy." The words still stung like a bull nettle. "In that instant I knew I'd be a yes-wife like Renee, always bowing to my husband's wishes. I wanted more. I wanted a man who would love me above everything, even his family. I took off the ring and gave it back, saying I couldn't marry him. I waited and waited for Judd to come and confess his undying love. I'm still waiting." She laughed, a pitiful sound that revealed how weak she felt.

"Oh, Cait. I didn't know." Maddie slipped from the chair and held her tightly.

"Me, neither." Sky hugged her in turn, then leaned away with a mischievous glint in her eyes. "You know, Cait, a woman has ways to bring a man to his knees."

"I think I missed that course in college."

"Oh, please." Sky undid a couple of snaps on Cait's shirt. "Get my drift?"

Caitlyn remembered yesterday, and how Judd had looked at her breasts. Oh, yeah, she got it. "So you don't want me to apologize?"

"Not on your life." Skylar laughed and held up her hand for a high five.

"I just need some time," Cait said. "Two weeks tops to find a solution."

"Okay," her sisters said in unison.

Cait prayed that somehow she could work out a plan to help them all.

CHAPTER EIGHT

"YOU'LL NEVER GUESS who I saw yesterday. The Belle sisters, all three of them. You know the other two are kind of like Caitlyn, uppity but with a northern flair. They never said a word to me. How rude is that? Believe me, Southerners have much better manners. But you know, if I had looks like that I wouldn't have to worry for the rest of my life. I'd be on easy street, with a rich hunk of my choosing. All I'd have to do is spend his money and look oh, so pretty. Now that I—"

"Brenda Sue!"

She jumped at the sound of his voice.

"Is there a reason you're in my study?" Judd asked, his tone peppered with impatience.

"Oh, you don't have to shout."

"And you need to take a breath."

"What?"

The woman looked genuinely puzzled. Did she not have a clue? Damn it! "What are you doing in my study? This isn't the office."

"Sometimes, Judd, you can be rude," she replied in a haughty tone.

He leaned back, her voice wearing holes in whatever patience he had left. "You have five seconds to tell me in one sentence what you're doing in here or you're fired. Is that rude enough for you?"

She flipped back her yellowish-blond hair. "Harland finished repairing the fence between the ranch and High Five, and wanted you to know. He double wired it or something, so the Belles' bull can't get onto Southern Cross. Why couldn't Caitlyn fix it? It seemed—"

Judd pointed to the door. "Go, as fast as you can."

She fled.

His mother walked through the open door, glancing at Brenda Sue's retreating figure. "Dare I ask if you made her mad enough to quit?"

"She has two kids. She needs a job."

"Mmm. What's wrong with this picture?"

"What do you mean?" He kept signing checks for bills. He usually did that in the office, but there was just so much of Brenda Sue he could tolerate on any given day.

"You keep her on and put up with her endless marathon of drivel because she needs a job. You better be careful or people might start calling you a nice guy."

He signed another check. "I did it as a favor to Harvey. Is there something you need?"

"Yes." His mother clasped her hands together. "As I'm sure Brenda Sue has relayed to you, the Belle sisters are here, and I want to throw a party. A ball, actually, with formal attire."

He glanced up. "Have you lost your mind?"

"No. My faculties are all intact, thank you. It'll be like the old days, when we had such wonderful parties at Southern Cross."

"No," he said, and went back to signing checks.

Renee yanked the pen from his hand. His brows knotted so tightly he could feel them almost meeting.

"We're having a party. Get used to the idea. And you're wearing your tuxedo. The first dance is with me. After that you can have your choice of all the nice young ladies who will be here. Think marriage. Think babies. Think of making your mama happy. Other than that, I don't want to hear a word out of you. Oh, and of course, write me a very big check. The ball will take place Saturday night, so I have to get moving."

He grabbed his pen from her hand. "You've been around Brenda Sue too long. You need to breathe when you're issuing orders and otherwise annoying the living hell out of me."

"We're having a party, Judd."

"Don't count on me being there." He signed yet another check with a flourish.

"Well, I suppose you don't have to attend. I'll invite sons of your father's friends who would love to dance with the Belle sisters."

"Whatever."

"Mmm. You and Caitlyn couldn't make it work. Have you thought of Madison or Skylar? Very striking women."

"I'm not in the market for a wife." He kept signing.

"I want grandbabies."

"Rent one."

"Write me a very fat check, then. Babies on the black market cost a fortune."

He turned the page in the checkbook. "Go away, Mom. This is getting tiring."

"There will be other women here besides the Belles. This is your night to choose, so you'd better make good use of it. I'll even buy a gown for Brenda Sue and trot her out."

He couldn't hide a grin. "You must be getting desperate."

"I am, and you already have one desperate woman on your tail. You certainly don't want another, especially when she's your mother."

"Okay. Okay." He threw the pen down. "Have the damn party."

His mom flew around the desk and hugged him. "You really are a sweetie."

He let that pass. "Nothing excessive."

"There's no fun in that. I'll just surprise you." She hurried to the door, and he wondered if she'd heard anything he said. "I'll take your tux to the cleaners, so don't worry about that."

"That's a load off my mind."

"Don't be sarcastic."

"Don't bother me, then," Judd muttered. But the doorway was empty.

He glanced down at the checks. Damn it! The last two he'd signed as "Caitlyn Belle." Ripping them out, he tore the checks into tiny pieces and swore a few more cuss words.

Judd stood and walked to the window, flexing his shoulders to relieve the tension. Ever since he'd seen Caitlyn yesterday, he hadn't been able to get her out of his mind. He wasn't a sentimental person; his father had made sure of that. Men didn't cry or show their emotions. It made them weak. And Jack Calhoun had wanted Judd to be strong. Strong enough to rule Southern Cross. Strong enough to marry the right woman to ensure the lineage of the Calhoun name.

You'll marry Caitlyn Belle. She's a fine woman and will produce strong sons. She's young and stubborn, but Dane will keep her in line. The union will make both families stronger.

At the time, Judd hadn't balked at the idea. He didn't believe in falling in love or living happily ever after. His mother had pretty much killed all those feelings when she'd left him alone, to be raised by a domineering father.

And Judd had been watching Caitlyn Belle for a long time. He'd thought she was too young for him, though; he liked his women more experienced. That didn't keep him from admiring her beauty when he saw her riding, her black hair flying in the wind. In tight jeans and an even tighter blouse, she sat a saddle better than any woman he'd ever seen.

She rode into his dreams many nights, beguiling, tempting him with her blue forget-me-not eyes, full lips and a body that was made for a man's enjoyment. Caitlyn could arouse him more in his thoughts than other women could in the flesh.

Marrying her wasn't a problem. It would be a pleasure. But she wanted something he wasn't willing to give her—couldn't give her. She wanted his love.

How could he tell her he didn't know anything about the fickle emotion? Nor did he want to learn. It only brought pain. To his shock, she'd walked away. He knew she'd come back, though. Dane would make her. And women did what men told them. His father had drilled that concept into him all his life.

But Caitlyn wasn't like a willow that bent easily. She was more like a mighty oak, and stood strong in her convictions. Ultimately, neither Dane nor his father could change her mind.

She either wanted to marry him or she didn't. That was Judd's bottom line.

He quirked his lips. Man, they had sexual chemistry, though. It was obvious every time he was around her. Kissing her, having sex with her could generate enough electricity to light up the Astrodome.

His gut tightened and he cursed again. Thoughts of her made him need a cold shower in the middle of the day.

He turned his attention to the sisters. Since Madison and Skylar didn't live here, he was almost positive they'd apply pressure to sell. How would Caitlyn handle that?

He'd used bravado when he'd talked about buying the royalties from Dane, claiming he would take everything she loved. Judd didn't quite understand why he felt he had to do that. Maybe because she actually *could* love, and he couldn't.

What was his success going to prove when it was all over? He would have money and power, but he wouldn't have her.

CAIT STARED AT RED as the horse threw up her head and neighed, clearly wanting to be ridden.

"She's a beautiful animal," Cooper said, leaning on the fence beside her.

"Yep. My dad knew horseflesh. She's all rippling muscle, and she rides faster and smoother than a brand-new Cadillac."

"Since you won't allow anyone else to ride her, I wouldn't know."

Cait yanked Coop's hat lower. "Don't give me that woebegone puppy-dog look. She's my horse and…"

He straightened his hat. "And what?"

"I have to sell her." The words went down like a jalapeño pepper, burning all the way.

"Whoa." Coop removed his hat and scratched his head. "Didn't see that one coming. You love that horse."

"I love Gran and High Five more."

Somewhere through her chaotic and tangled thoughts, she knew what she had to do. Besides High Five, Whiskey Red was the only thing of value she owned.

Coop settled his hat on his head with a wry expression. "Your sisters have something to do with that decision?"

"I'm asking them to make sacrifices, so I have to be willing to do the same."

"Mmm."

All her life she had thought her sisters were living a fairy tale, with luxury at their fingertips. The truth was so different than what she'd imagined. They had heartaches and problems, too.

As much as she hated to let Red go, she knew it was the only way to help Maddie and Sky. The sale would give them money to live on, and Cait time to form a plan to save the ranch. It would solve their problems for now.

"I'm setting the sale for Friday at ten. Tell Rufus to get the word out to all the horse people who might be interested. I'll make a few calls, too."

"That's mighty quick."

"Yeah." Her gaze swung to Red again. *Sorry, girl.* "I better make those calls." She hurried toward the house.

"Cait?"

She turned, shading her eyes against the glare of the sun.

"I'm sorry."

She nodded and continued on her way. Tears stung the back of her eyes and she knew this was the start of Judd taking everything she loved. He wasn't taking Red; Cait was selling her.

But somehow it felt the same.

PHOTO ALBUMS AND PICTURES were strewn all over the parlor. Whenever her sisters came home,

Gran's favorite thing was to reminisce about their childhood and happier times.

"Caitlyn, come look," her grandmother said. "We're having so much fun."

She sat on the sofa. Maddie and Sky were at her feet, albums in their laps. Cait plopped down to join them. She'd worry later.

They were giggling over the frizzy red hair Sky had had as a child when there was a knock at the door. Cait pushed herself to her feet. "I'll get it."

She swung open the door and shock ran through her. Renee Calhoun stood there, dressed to the nines in a pale pink linen pantsuit and heels. Her blond hair hung in a pageboy around her face. Judd looked nothing like his beautiful mother. He favored his father, with chiseled features and a dark, brooding personality.

"Caitlyn, dear, it's so good to see you."

Cait inclined her head, feeling a knot the size of a baseball forming in her stomach. "What can I do for you, Mrs. Calhoun?"

"Oh, please. You used to call me Renee."

"That was a long time ago." She kept her voice neutral, wondering what the woman wanted.

Renee touched her arm. "Too long, my dear." She looked past Cait. "Is your grandmother home?"

The knot expanded. "Yes, but—"

"Relax, Caitlyn. This will only take a minute

and it'll be painless." Before Cait could stop her, Renee marched into the parlor.

Damn woman. What did she want?

Cait hurried after her. Maddie and Sky got to their feet. Gran stared at Renee with a startled expression.

"Dorie, I'm sorry for intruding."

"Oh, Renee." Gran shook her head as if to clear it, then patted the cushion. "Sit down, please. You've met my granddaughters."

"Oh, yes. Many times." She settled on the sofa and placed her bag beside her. "Very beautiful young women."

Maddie eased down on the other side of Gran, who reached for her hand. "I've been very blessed," the elderly woman said. "My granddaughters are a special gift from my son."

A look of discomfort crossed Renee's face. "I am so sorry about Dane."

"Thank you." Gran nodded and dropped her gaze.

Cait wanted to rush in and stop whatever was about to happen. Anything to protect Gran. But she didn't believe, not for one minute, that Renee would intentionally hurt her grandmother.

Their visitor pulled an ivory linen envelope from her purse. "I have some exciting news. I'm throwing a big party—a ball with formal attire— and I would love for you and your lovely granddaughters to attend."

A ball! Was the woman out of her mind?

Gran raised one hand to her breasts. "A party? Oh, my, we haven't had a party in ages."

Not since Caitlyn and Judd's engagement party. Everyone was thinking it, but no one said the words out loud. If they did, Cait was going to hurt them.

"It sounds like a very nice party." Sky picked up an album and laid it on a table. "But I'm leaving early Sunday morning."

"The party is Saturday evening, so you have plenty of time. It will be fun—something we all need."

"Thank you for the invitation, but I didn't bring any clothes to wear to a fancy ball." Maddie smiled politely.

Cait thought it was time to step in. "I'm sorry, Renee, but neither my sisters nor I will be attending any party at Southern Cross. I'm sure you understand." She headed for the kitchen to ease the knot in her stomach.

"Caitlyn Dane Belle!"

Gran's voice stopped her as effectively as a bullet. Her tone had the power to squeeze the stubbornness right out of her.

"We do not treat guests in our home that way."

Like a dutiful granddaughter, Cait turned and faced the woman who meant more to her than life itself.

"Yes, ma'am."

Sometimes Gran's Southern manners grated on her nerves like a squeaky screen door. But Cait would never show her any disrespect.

Gran rose to her full height, which was barely five feet three inches. "Our neighbor has invited us to a fancy party and, as good neighbors, we will accept."

Like hell. Cait stopped the words just in time. Gran didn't know about the latest incident with the Calhouns, and Cait couldn't tell her. She caught the glint in Renee's eyes. Oh, Judd's mother was counting on that. Conniving witch.

Gran walked to Caitlyn and linked her arm through hers. "You work too hard. You need some fun." She patted her hand. "This is what you need, my baby. We'll get all dressed up and have the time of our lives."

"Gran..." She wanted to shout that the party wasn't about dressing up or Southern manners. It was about a black-hearted devil trying to steal High Five.

As if she understood Cait's hesitation, Dorie said, "I know Judd will be there, but it's been a long time. We're neighbors, so we have to be civil."

"Oh, this is wonderful." Renee rose to her feet. "I look forward to seeing you all. Ta-ta."

Caitlyn beat her to the door. "What are you trying to pull? We are not attending any stupid ball."

Renee tapped a French manicured nail against her lips. "Judd said the same thing."

"Then why are you doing this?"

"For fun."

"For fun?" She arched an eyebrow. "How about spite?"

"Now, Caitlyn…"

"Haven't you Calhouns hurt us enough? What else can you take from me?"

Renee slipped her bag over her shoulder. "Maybe I'm trying to give you something back." After delivering that ridiculous message, she sashayed out to her car.

Cait slammed the door so hard her ancestors could hear the echo.

CHAPTER NINE

THE NEXT TWO DAYS were hectic as Caitlyn ran the ranch and tried to get ready for Friday's sale. It helped that Maddie and Sky were home. She didn't have to run back to the house to check on Gran. Her sisters took very good care of her, and Dorie was happy.

They'd decided not to mention the ball again in hopes she would forget about it. Attending wasn't in their plans.

The day was hot and Cait felt sweat trickling down her back and staining her clothes. She smelled as fresh as cow manure.

Coop and Rufus had cut the hay three days ago. It was now cured, so they were racking it into windrows to bale. There were three one-hundred-acre tracts of coastal, and it would take them at least the month of June, if not more, to get all the hay off the ground.

But they'd have enough to see them through a dry summer and a bad winter. She planned to sell what she didn't need. That would help with expenses.

While Coop and Rufus worked with the hay, she took care of the cattle. Since it was already getting dry, she had to keep a close watch on the stock tanks, wells and windmills. It was crucial that the herds had water, especially in this heat.

It was getting late and Cait had one more windmill to check. She was so ready to head back to the air-conditioned ranch house and a bath.

But something was wrong. She knew that the moment she saw the cows huddled around the trough, bellowing. She rode in quickly, the dogs trotting behind her, and the animals scattered. Dismounting, she saw the trough was empty. That meant the storage tank was empty, too. Damn!

Glancing up, she watched the windmill's blades spinning in the breeze. But water wasn't pouring out of the pipe from the storage tank, as per normal.

It was a long way up the tower. Cait felt dizzy just looking upward. This had happened about three weeks ago, when the clevis and cotter pins had been broken. Could it be the same problem? She didn't understand how they could break again so soon. She had no recourse but to climb the tower to find out why the sucker rod wasn't pumping water into the trough.

Either that or the leathers needed changing. She'd have to call someone to repair that. If the gears or the pump were broken, fixing them would be a big expense.

A cow butted her, sending Cait staggering. "Be patient, old gal. I'll see what I can do, and stop pushing me around. I'm your only salvation." She whistled for the dogs and they responded, yapping and nipping at the cows until they shuffled away from the trough.

Cait searched her saddlebags for cotter and clevis pins. She'd bought some when the device had broken last time. If that was the problem, she could easily fix it.

On the horizon, beyond the High Five fence line, she glimpsed Southern Cross cowboys. Had they sabotaged the windmill? She wouldn't put it past them. And she wouldn't put it past Judd.

She found the pins and stuffed them into her jeans pocket. Glancing up, she trembled. She wasn't afraid of heights. Normal heights, that is. But the tower had to be at least forty feet high, and was old and shaky. She always felt a little jittery when she had to climb it.

The cattle needed water, however, so she tucked away her fears and marched to the tower.

Reaching it, she yanked off her shirt. She would need her arms free and unrestricted.

Luckily, she had a white cotton tank top on underneath.

The dogs dutifully worked the cattle, keeping them away as Cait placed a booted foot on the first steel rung of the ladder and started up. The sun torched her skin, but she kept climbing, staying focused and not looking down. She felt as if she were climbing into a hot tunnel of hell.

Reaching the hub, she took care not to get her head or anything else she might need chopped off. Quickly, Cait pulled the brake to stop the blades. The swooshing sound died away.

Don't look down.

Her breathing was labored, but that was normal under the circumstances. She concentrated on the C-shaped shackle that worked the sucker rod. It was missing both pins. Damn! She'd found the problem. Now to fix it.

Holding on with one hand, she slipped the other in her pocket for the pins. The clevis consisted of a head, shank and hole. The cotter pin went through the hole to hold it in place. She placed the cotter pin between her teeth.

Stretching out her arm, she grabbed the shackle and inserted the clevis, or at least tried. It was stubborn and didn't budge. Cait shoved with all her might, trying to position it back in place so she could insert the cotter pin.

The wind blew off her hat and fear tightened her throat, but she didn't lose her concentration. Nor did she look down.

"Come on, you stupid pin. Move." With all her strength she pushed until it slid into place, all the while trying to keep her balance. It took every muscle she had to hold it there as she slipped the cotter pin through the hole. Then and only then did she take a breath, scraping precious air from the bottom of her lungs.

The wind tugged and she quickly released the brake, waiting as the blades revved up again. Slowly the sucker rod began to move up and down, hopefully pumping water from beneath the ground into the storage tank, and then into the trough. Cait didn't see if it was happening, because she refused to look down. She'd find out soon enough….

Now she had to climb down. But first she had to loosen her grip and move her feet. One, two, three… She lowered one foot and then the other. All the way to the precious earth, which she wanted to kiss the moment her boots touched it.

But she had other problems. The water was not going into the trough. The cows must have dislocated a pipe, and water was spurting everywhere.

Damn! Damn! Damn!

JUDD WATCHED HER from a hill and had no intention of helping or interfering. But he could see water puddling on the ground, the sun glistening off its surface. The cows bellowed, shifting restlessly, and though the dogs worked to keep them at bay, the big animals smelled water. The dogs would not hold them long.

Without a second thought, Judd jumped Baron over the fence onto the High Five ranch. He gave the horse his lead and they flew over the dried grass. As he neared the windmill, cattle broke free, running and bellowing for the water.

Caitlyn glanced at the stampeding cows and made a dash for her horse, just as Judd swept in, grabbed her around the waist and rode to safety.

"Let me go," she screeched, her heart pounding against his hand. His fingers touched the underside of her breast, and even riding full tilt, he felt a powerful response.

"Let me go!" She flailed her arms, and he pulled up and released her. Cait fell to the ground on her butt, her eyes firing blue flames at him. "You bastard."

He sat back in the saddle, staring down at her. "Is that any way to talk to a man who just saved your life?"

She stood and dusted off the back of her jeans. "You're trespassing, Judd. Get off my property."

She swung her cute butt around and headed back to the cattle jostling around the trough, fighting to get a drink of water.

Placing two fingers in her mouth, she whistled. The dogs trotted over, looking eagerly up at her. "Go. Go. Go." She clapped her hands. "Get 'em."

In a frenzy, the dogs went after the cows, herding them away from the trough once more. Caitlyn stepped into the mud without hesitation and bent to a pipe that was gushing water.

Judd slid from the saddle and went to help her. His head told him to ride away; this woman had hurt him more than anyone in his life. But his heart was a traitor, urging him forward.

The pipe ran along the ground and up into the trough. The top part had come undone. Caitlyn grabbed the pipe to force it back in place, but the water pressure made that difficult. Judd placed his hands over hers and pushed.

She stilled for a moment and he expected more fireworks, but her fingers tightened under his and the two of them pushed together. Water squirted him in the face and chest, as it did her, but they focused on their goal. Neither spoke. The stubborn pipe finally moved into the trough and water spilled into its depth.

Caitlyn let out a sigh and wiped water from her cheeks. Her eyes pinned him like a target to a wall. "I didn't ask for your help, so please leave. You're not welcome here." Her words were like darts. If he was a soft man, they might hurt, but they didn't. They only irritated him.

"I thought your grandmother had at least taught you some manners. And she should have told you not to climb a windmill out here when no one is around."

"Evidently someone was, and I'm wondering why all of a sudden you're on High Five. And your cowboys. I saw them a little while ago. I'm beginning to think maybe the cotter pin was taken out."

He straightened. "Are you accusing me of deliberately breaking the windmill?"

Her eyes zoomed to his. "Maybe."

"Caitlyn, I don't have to sabotage you. You'll fail all on your own. Even Dane knew that."

"Don't say one word about my father." Her chest swelled with anger and her breasts pressed against the tank top. Since it was wet, he saw just about everything, and felt that familiar kick in his groin. That irritated him more.

The cows began to outmaneuver the dogs again, hurrying to the water. One rushed in and bumped Caitlyn, and she landed on her back in the mud, arms and legs flying.

Once Judd saw that she was okay, he wanted to

laugh, which he did. Not much, just a chuckle he couldn't suppress. Mud caked her body, her skin.

Her face froze into a mask of disbelief.

More cows made their way to the trough. He'd help her, but he knew she didn't want his assistance. "Get up or you're going to get trampled."

She rose to her hands and knees, and flipped and flopped like a beetle on its back. Unable to stand the sight a moment longer, he stretched out his hand. She didn't take it.

"Don't be a stubborn fool."

She latched on to it then and yanked. He went flying into the muck beside her. That, he didn't find funny. Mud soaked his clothes. His boots! He groaned. His favorite boots were ruined.

"Why aren't you laughing?" she asked, leaning back in the mud as if it were whipped cream. And she was the cat who had just had her fill.

He slipped and slid, but managed to get to his feet and to solid ground. Using the trough for leverage, she pulled herself up and waded out as well.

"You need a damn good spanking." The words were out before he could corral them.

She cocked her head, water dripping from her braid and other parts of her body. "A little mud make you cranky?" Her eyes slid down his body to his crotch. "Or horny?"

Before he knew what he was doing, he'd jerked

her into his arms. Their mud-coated bodies welded together, every soft curve of hers pressed into his hardness, and he wanted her more than he ever had.

Her open mouth was a breath away. Her tongue touched her upper lip, and he realized she was the one in control, taking him places he'd sworn he'd never go again.

With more restraint than he knew he had, he pushed her away and strolled to his horse.

"Stay off my property, Judd Calhoun," she shouted after him.

He swung into the saddle, cursing. Baron pranced around and Judd rode to within a few feet of her.

"It won't be yours long, Caitlyn. Not for long."

"Go to hell!" Her words carried on the wind as he galloped away.

AIR GUSHED INTO Cait's lungs, hot and furious, just the way Judd made her feel. How dare he! As the anger oozed out of her, her heart rate returned to normal. Or as close as it was going to get today.

She glanced down at her mud-covered body and felt Judd's male imprint there. Her nipples hardened and her lower abdomen ached. Oh, she was so easy. All he had to do was kiss her… But he hadn't. Her mouth watered for what she'd been deprived of. It felt good, though, to know she had some power over him. Still.

Maybe Sky was right.

Could Cait work this to her advantage? It would be like sleeping with the enemy, and that had to be bad. Though her body was telling her something else...

Mooing cows brought her out of her insanity. They were fighting to get to the trough, butting heads. She clapped her hands again. "Go, go, boys."

The dogs went back into action, keeping the cattle busy and frustrated while the trough filled up. Finally satisfied they had enough water, she plucked her shirt and hat from the mud. They were ruined, but she couldn't leave them out here. The cows, being very curious, would try to make a snack out of the items.

With her shirt and hat rolled into a ball, she climbed into the saddle and headed for home.

THE SALE WAS Friday morning and Cait put the encounter with Judd out of her mind. Or at least she tried.

Coop wanted to stay and help, but she needed him in the hay field. Soon trucks pulling trailers nosed up to the fence at the corral. Her father's poker buddies hadn't let her down; they were here in full force. Red would bring a good price. But her heart was breaking. That, she wouldn't let anyone see.

Maddie hugged her. "I'm sorry you have to sell Red."

"It's to help us all." The three sisters stood in the barn and Cait rubbed Red down for the last time. The thoroughbred's muscles rippled and her coat was shiny. Someone would get a very good horse.

Sky stroked Red's long neck. "I wish there was another way."

"There isn't, so let's be big girls and pull up our panties and get this done."

They laughed at one of Gran's sayings from their childhood. That Cait could join in was a good sign. She'd survive this.

She held Whiskey Red's face and kissed her nose. "Goodbye, girl." Swallowing her emotions, she took the bridle and led her into the corral.

Six buyers walked around Red, running their hands along her back, her butt, her neck, her legs.

Red threw up her head and neighed, clearly not liking this inspection. "Easy, girl," Cait soothed.

"She's a fine looking animal," Dale Eddy said, chewing on a cigar.

"Yes, she is," Cait replied. "Let's get the bidding started."

"Twenty thousand." Dale made the first offer.

Bill Lightfoot eyed the column of Red's strong neck. "Twenty-five."

"Thirty." Dale upped his bid.

"Thirty-five," Charley Bowers said.

Frank Upton shook his head. "Too rich for my blood."

"Forty." Dale bid again, the cigar working overtime. Caitlyn knew he really wanted Red, and the horse would have a good home at Dale's ranch.

Bob O'Neal had walked around Red several times, but hadn't yet bid. "Forty-five," he said suddenly.

This was going better than Cait had expected. She'd been hoping for forty. More would make life a lot easier.

"Seventy-five thousand dollars."

Cait swung her head in the direction of the voice. No! He couldn't take Red. Not Judd. She wouldn't allow it.

"She's not for sale to you."

Judd walked farther into the corral. "So you posted the sale in bad faith?"

Maddie and Sky came to stand beside her. Cait thought of Kira, of Maddie's medical bills and her own pride. She had no choice. A buyer was a buyer. Even if he was the devil.

"You don't have to do this," Sky said in a whisper.

But Cait did. She couldn't renege on a sale, and they needed the money, even if it came from Judd Calhoun.

"No." Pride went down hard and bitter. "Red is for sale."

Judd looked at the other men. "Anyone want to top my bid?"

Dale patted Red's rump. "I was there the day Dane bought this horse. She has great bloodlines and she's worth every penny."

"That's not a bid, Dale," Judd told him.

The man shook his head. "That's out of my price range."

The others walked off and Caitlyn faced Judd. Maddie and Sky stood behind her like her wingmen.

"Why are you doing this?" she asked as calmly as she could.

"I can never pass up good horseflesh."

"Or sticking it to me."

He nodded. "That's always a plus."

Sky stepped forward. "You've gotten hard, Judd."

"Hello, Sky, Maddie." He tipped his hat. "I had a very good teacher."

"Oh, please, no one had to teach you a thing."

Cait placed a hand on Sky's arm before her sister went on full alert. "He's paying a lot of money for Red. Money we need." Her eyes probed the dark depths of his. "I find that a little strange. You're giving me money to succeed."

"But I'm taking something you love." His gaze never wavered as he delivered a blow that left her speechless. She found there was no response, other than to burst into tears. And she would never do that.

"I'd like a cashier's check by the end of the day."

He seemed taken aback. "Don't you trust me?"

When she didn't respond, he shrugged. "I'll have a check and a trailer here later."

"If you don't, the sale is off."

She watched as he walked out of the corral. He went to the end of the barn, where his horse was tethered. No wonder she hadn't heard him arrive. Sneaky devil!

But his scheme had started.

Would he completely destroy her?

CHAPTER TEN

JUDD WALKED IN the back door and stopped short. People were everywhere. People he didn't know. Damn party! He made his way down the hall toward his study, sidestepping tables, chairs and startled maids.

His mother hurried from the dining room. "Oh, Judd…"

"Do you really need all this help to get ready for a party?"

Renee glanced at the women arranging flowers in the entry. "Why, of course. We need decorators, caterers, maids and servers. Several guests will be spending the night."

He shook his head and went into his study. "Keep everyone, and I mean everyone, out of my space."

As always, his mother paid him no attention and followed him.

"Everyone meant you, too, Mom." He sank into his leather chair.

"Did I see Harland unloading that beautiful red horse of Caitlyn's?"

"Yes." Judd picked up his mail.

"Why is it here?"

"I bought her."

"What?"

He laid down his mail. "Don't you have a party to plan?"

Renee closed the door and walked to his desk. "Now, let me get this straight. Caitlyn put her horse up for sale and you bought it. I'm guessing at a very high price."

"You got it."

"Why, son? Why would you do that? It doesn't make any sense."

"It doesn't have to."

"This woman you want to bring down. This woman who hurt you. You're now giving her money."

"I bought a good horse. That's it. I'm getting tired of this interrogation." He rose to his feet and shoved his hands into his pockets.

"Son…"

"It wasn't about the money, okay? I took something she loved."

"Oh, well, that's just dandy," Renee said, narrowing her green eyes on his face. He hated when she did that. He didn't want her to see too much. "You're not this hard."

He moved toward the window. "You don't really know me."

"It all comes back to the bad mother, doesn't it?"

"Leave it alone, Mom."

"I can't when it's destroying your whole life."

"Mom…"

"I've told you a million times, I had to go in order to survive. I never planned to leave you here. I had you in my arms, but Jack ripped you away. When I tried to stay then, he forced me out. I had no choice. I left, but I fully intended to get custody. I never counted on your father's vindictiveness."

Judd clenched his jaw. "I've heard this story before."

"I tried twice to kidnap you. I even made it to the upstairs landing the second time before I was caught."

"What?" He swung around. "I never knew that. Dad said you never came back."

"Your father was very good at turning every situation to his advantage."

Judd removed his hat and placed it carefully on his desk. "I'll never understand why you married him again."

"Yes, you do. I've told you many times. When your father came into that diner where I was working, I was a bit nervous. But the moment he showed he was still interested, I worked it to my advantage. I learned from him. I'd have done anything to be back with my son. And I did."

Judd raked his fingers through his hair. He didn't want to hear this story, and didn't understand why he was still listening.

"The marriage worked out well, though. Jack had mellowed and we formed a stronger relationship. That's the funny thing about love. Once it's given it's almost impossible to destroy."

Judd didn't have anything to say, and a response didn't seem to be required.

"You're the casualty of our dysfunctional lives. Jack filled your head with his misguided, outdated views of women, and sadly, nothing I said or tried to do changed your thinking. But deep down I know you're a caring, compassionate man who can love deeply."

He had his doubts about that. He flung a hand toward the door. "Go plan your party, and stop spending so damn much money."

His mother lifted her chin. "I'll spend however much I please. Since you've irritated Caitlyn, the Belles probably won't come. It's not going to be much of a party without them."

"Good. Then we can forget this whole crazy idea."

"Not on your life. I bought this beautiful gold gown and I'm wearing it." She cocked her head. "I see myself as a fairy godmother."

"I see you as insane."

"Tut-tut." She shook a finger at him. "Don't talk like that to your mother."

He sighed. "You try my patience, you know that?"

"Yes, my dear son." She turned toward the door, then swung back. "I do love you, Judd, and Caitlyn did, too. One day you're going to realize that, and I hope it's not too late."

He plopped back into his chair as her words hit him right between the eyes. *Love?* Why did women brandish that word like a weapon? They wanted everything wrapped in a neat package with *married* and *happily ever after* written on it. But it never turned out that way. There always seemed to be more pain than happiness. A cynical outlook, perhaps, but he was a cynical, unfeeling man. That's the way Caitlyn thought of him.

Time and again he'd proved he could feel deeply—sexually. But she wanted the package with the vows of undying love.

He shifted restlessly. Their encounter at the windmill epitomized their relationship. They both felt a powerful attraction. Why wasn't that enough for her? It was for him.

Damn. He flexed his shoulders. He was so tired

of thinking of her. When he'd heard of the sale, he'd had no intention of buying her horse. He had all the horses he needed, but against every sane thought in his head, he'd found his way there.

Another way to stick it to me.

Maybe. He wasn't quite sure why he'd done it. All he knew was that he could and he had. Maybe it was a way to regain some of the ground she'd stolen at the windmill. Even he had to admit that little by little she was making inroads into his control. Into his resolve.

She made him weak when he wanted to be strong. She made him caring when he wanted to be tough. She made him feel pain when he wanted to be oblivious.

But he was never oblivious to her.

He could still see the hurt in her eyes when he'd bought Whiskey Red. That's what he wanted, wasn't it? Where was his feeling of victory?

"Judd."

He turned around and tried not to groan at Brenda Sue's interruption.

"My goodness, it's hard not to trip over maids, florists and whoever these people are. Your mother didn't ask for my opinion. She can be rather snotty sometimes. I don't think she likes me, but gosh, she knows how to throw a party. Crystal, flowers and a band—the whole nine yards. No plastic at this shindig. Everything is oh, so nice, and you should see the flower arrangement in the foyer. I could live a week on what that cost. But I've never—"

"Brenda Sue." Judd had to shout to get her attention. "Is there a reason you're in my study—again?"

She blinked like a raccoon with a light shining in its face. "Oh—oh, yes. Harland sent me to tell you that the new horse…" She wrinkled her nose. "Isn't that Caitlyn's horse? Sure looks like it. Anyway, Harland said the horse is not settling down, and he wants to know if you want him to give her something to calm her. Like, wow, I didn't even know you could do that. How…"

Judd grabbed his hat and hit the door, leaving Brenda Sue in midsentence. It would probably be five minutes before she realized he wasn't there.

He ran out the back and headed for the stables. No one was touching that horse. No one was touching Whiskey Red but him.

Caitlyn couldn't sleep. She kept wondering how Red was adjusting to the stables at Southern Cross. She was a thoroughbred and temperamental, but Cait was sure Judd had professional people to deal with her. That didn't make her feel better, though.

She'd received the payment early enough to go into Giddings and deposit the money. When

Maddie and Sky left on Sunday, she'd write them each a check for their part. Her share would go back into the ranch.

It was a solution for now.

She was up the next morning before everyone. She grabbed some cereal bars and bottled water and headed for the bunkhouse. Today would be a full day of baling hay.

Rufus ran the tractor with the baler. It would break every now and then, but she knew the two ranch hands could fix it. Cooper worked the hay carrier that loaded each bale and carted it to a fence line, where it would be stacked until it was sold or fed to the cattle.

Cooper and Rufus had a system, so Caitlyn soon left to check the herds.

The windmill was working fine, the trough full of water. She stared at the mud puddle and briefly thought of yesterday.

And Judd.

He'd seemed to want to help, but then he... She shut out the memory and went on to the next pasture.

This one had a stock tank and it was already getting low. A good rain would help tremendously. The summers were always hell. But then the winters weren't a picnic, either.

Ranching was tough on a good day, and she

wondered why she was killing herself to preserve something no one cared about but her. She knew, though. *For Gran. For her heritage.* Gran was the only mother Cait had ever known, and she would do everything to keep her on High Five.

The royalty sale ensured that Dorie could stay at the ranch until her death. But what would that be like for her? Dorie's childhood home would no longer be High Five, but part of the Southern Cross. Once Gran knew that, she wouldn't stay in the house. Cait knew her grandmother's pride wouldn't let her.

Somehow Caitlyn had to make the ranch work.

By the time Cait reached home that evening, she was exhausted. She wanted a bath, some food and...

She paused in the kitchen doorway. Etta, Maddie and Sky stood there, looking anxious.

Cait whipped off her hat. "What's wrong? Is it Gran?"

"Where have you been? It's six o'clock." Sky didn't bother to hide her temper.

"Where do you think I've been? I'm working this ranch."

"Calm down." Maddie was quick to intervene.

"You girls better get a move on," Etta said. "Miss Dorie doesn't like to be late."

"Late? For what?"

"Have you forgotten what today is?" Sky

asked, rather tartly. At Cait's blank look, she added, "The ball."

Caitlyn frowned. "I'm not going to that. I refuse to. No way in hell can anyone make me."

"Go upstairs and tell your grandmother." Etta removed her apron. "I'm heading home. Food's in the refrigerator."

As the housekeeper went out the screen door, Maddie and Sky grabbed Cait by her arms and pulled her toward the staircase.

"What are you doing?"

"I'm going to make this short and sweet," Sky said as they climbed the stairs. "Renee called this morning to make sure we were coming, and Gran's been in a tizzy all day getting ready."

"What?"

"Oh, yeah." Maddie opened the door. "Wait till you see."

Cait stood aghast at the chaos in Gran's room. Gowns were everywhere, strewn over chairs, the lounger and the bed. The same with shoes.

The elderly woman came from the bathroom in a long slip, patting her hair, which was in an elegant knot at her nape. "Oh, Caitlyn, baby," she said when she saw her. "Go take a bath. We don't have much time. Your dress is all ready."

"Welcome to bizarro world," Sky whispered.

"Wait till you see the dress." Maddie nudged her.

"I can't believe you couldn't dissuade her from this," Cait muttered with a touch of anger. "We're not going."

Sky lifted an eyebrow. "Tell Gran that, Miss Can-Do-Everything."

Cait shot her a thousand-watt glare and walked to Dorie, who was inspecting a silver, satiny creation.

"Gran." She spoke softly.

Her grandmother blinked at her. "Caitlyn, go take a bath. How many times do I have to tell you?"

She caught her hands. "Gran, listen to me. We're not going to any party at the Southern Cross."

"Oh, my baby." Gran cupped Cait's face in frail fingers, but Cait only felt their power. "I know you don't want to see Judd, but my precious, you made the choice long ago. And I know my baby has the strength to hold her head up and be a lady. To be a Belle. With Southern manners."

All her *no*s deflated into a big *oh*. She could hold her head up and face anybody, but she didn't want to go to the Calhouns' ranch. How could she get through to Gran?

"Gran, I'm tired. I've been working all day and I don't have a thing to wear."

Behind her, Sky snickered. That was not the right thing to say in a room full of gowns.

"I don't know why you fool around on the ranch.

Your father encouraged that and I never liked it. Leave the ranch to Dane. He runs it effortlessly."

Oh, God. Not today. Cait didn't want to say those words today.

Maddie put an arm around their grandmother's shoulders. "Gran, Dad is dead. He can't run the ranch."

"I know that." Dorie turned and picked up a gown from the bed. "Here's your dress, Caitlyn. I've already chosen it for you."

Cait stared at the garment. Staring was all she could do. It was red, strapless and tight fitting, with a slit up one leg.

"Daring little number, isn't it?" Sky said, tongue in cheek.

"Now, my babies, I'm going to finish my makeup, and you get dressed. Hurry."

The three of them stared at her as she closed the bathroom door.

"You handled that very well," Sky said, holding up the red dress with a lifted brow.

"I'm not going and I'm not wearing that. I'll look like a hooker."

Maddie reached for a white gown trimmed in pink, with capped sleeves and a full skirt. "Does this say Barbie? Virginal?"

Cait choked back a laugh even though there was nothing funny about this situation.

"Wait for this." Sky leaned over and plucked a black gown from the mix on the bed. "Does this say matronly?" It was a very simple sleeveless, long black dress with a V neckline. "Gran says I can wear a strand of her pearls. Oh, yeah, I'm going to party hearty."

Cait sank onto the bed, not caring about the gowns. "I don't know what to do."

Sky sat beside her, frowning at the black number. "We can just refuse to go. We're grown women and Gran can't force us."

"Yeah." Cait looked into Sky's eyes. "But are you willing to hurt her like that?"

"I'm not," Maddie said, plopping down beside them. "I'll wear this nightmare and smile, as long as it makes her happy."

"I think that's our bottom line," Cait murmured.

She hadn't thought about the ball all day, never had any intention of stepping foot onto Southern Cross property. But she had to give Renee credit. The conniving witch had found a way to get the Belles to the ball.

CHAPTER ELEVEN

CAIT WANTED TO LINGER in the bath, but she didn't have time. Damn party! Whoever heard of having a ball in Texas? She griped to herself the whole time she was dressing.

She lathered herself in scented lotion called *Moonlight Madness*. She was feeling a little mad tonight. The red dress lay on the bed. Strapless. It had been ages since she'd worn anything like that. Probably since college.

She dug in her dresser drawers until she found what she wanted—a strapless, push-up bra. A little old, but it still worked. She shimmied into it just as Maddie and Sky walked in dressed in their gowns, their faces somber.

"Hey, you don't look all that bad," she said. "Actually, you look damn good." She cast a not-so-nice glance at the red number. "I don't know how I'm going to hold up my dress."

"By those babes poking out of your chest there," Sky told her.

"Very funny." She grabbed the dress. "It's too revealing. It's not me."

"And you think this black nightmare is me?"

Cait looked her up and down. "Yeah. It's sassy and tempting, just revealing enough."

"Compliments won't work." Sky shoved the red dress into her hands. "Put it on."

Cait made a face and stared at the crimson fabric before wiggling into it. She held her breath and Maddie zipped her up. After shifting her breasts into the right position, she glanced in the mirror.

OhmyGod!

"Wow," Maddie said. "You look…"

"Like a hooker."

"No, sexy and wild, with your black hair hanging down your back like that."

"We need to do something with your mop." Sky grabbed a brush and wielded it through her locks.

"Ouch," she cried, and yanked the brush away. "I can fix my own damn hairdo, thank you." Then she smiled. "Remember all the times we did each other's hair?"

"Yeah," Maddie replied wistfully.

"Come on, you two," Sky urged. "We don't have time to go down memory lane. We're running late."

"Put your hair up," Maddie suggested. "It will look better that way."

Since Cait wore it in a braid most of the time,

it was wavy and easy to loop into a knot of curls on top of her head. Several strands hung loose around her face. Good enough.

She put diamond studs, a gift from her father, into her ears and stood. The dress covered her feet. "Oh, crap. This skirt is too long."

"No problem." Maddie handed her four-inch-high red heels.

Slipping them on, Cait asked, "Where does Gran get all this stuff?"

"From the trunks in the attic." Maddie held up her skirt to glance at her own shoes. "Mine are outdated, and so are yours, but who's going to notice?"

Thirty minutes later, they drove the Lincoln up the driveway at Southern Cross, Caitlyn at the wheel. The place was ablaze like Christmas at Graceland. Decorative lights lined the front of the house, but Cait didn't feel festive. She was more in the mood for a funeral.

A young man in black slacks and a white shirt came to her door with a big grin. Good grief, Renee had guys parking cars, probably in a cow pasture. Oh, yeah, this was Texas.

"Help Maddie with Gran," Cait said to Sky. "I'll have my hands full holding up this dress."

"Will you give it a rest?" Sky slipped a small beaded bag over her wrist. "You have plenty to hold it up. It's not like the summer we stuffed you with tissue."

Cait smiled as she slid out of the car, remembering her sixteenth birthday party. Breastwise, she'd grown since then, but at times she still felt like that young girl trying to prove she was a woman. To herself. Her father. Everyone.

She caught the boy staring at her skirt. The slit was cut up to way-past-decent and showed a lot of leg. Caitlyn handed him the keys. He kept staring. She wiggled them in front of his face. With a bashful grin, he grabbed them.

The little encounter gave her a burst of confidence. She could do this. If Judd could stick it to her, then she could stick it to him, even if she looked like something out of a 1950s movie. A sexy 1950s movie—with a streetwalker as a heroine.

They made their way up the walk, Maddie and Sky flanking Gran. Cait trailed behind with a sense of trepidation and excitement.

Renee was at the door, greeting guests, as they arrived. She looked years younger in a gold gossamer creation with a boat neck and sheer sleeves. The diamond pendant sparkling around her neck could support a family for a year.

The foyer showcased a huge flower arrangement, the fragrance of which wafted around them. For some reason it made Cait think of a night in the Garden of Eden. She knew the serpent was not far away.

But Judd was not standing with his mother.

"Oh, Dorie." Renee gave her grandmother an air hug. "I'm so glad you're here." Her gaze swung to the sisters. "And your granddaughters are lovely."

"Thank you. I'm very proud of them."

Renee's eyes settled on Caitlyn. "Oh, my dear. I wish I was young enough to wear red."

Did that require a response? Cait didn't think so.

"There's plenty of food and drink. Enjoy yourselves."

They trailed into the party room, speaking to neighbors as they went. A band played softly in the background. A buffet was set up at one end of the room, and guests milled around it. Tables bedecked with white linens and centerpieces of azalea sprigs and tea-light candles floating in crystal bowls were placed around the room. The double French doors were flung open, with more tables outside.

A déjà vu feeling came over Caitlyn. This was almost identical to their engagement party fourteen years ago. She'd been young and so much in love. She'd thought she'd found her prince. She'd thought he loved her.

But he'd only desired her.

Just as she was sinking into despair, Sky grabbed her arm. "We found a table. Let's get some food. Remember at your engagement party they had all those delicious appetizers? I hope they have some tonight."

"Could we not talk about my engagement party, please?"

"Touchy subject, huh?" Sky looked around. "I wonder where Judd is?"

"Maybe he has enough sense to stay away."

"Caitlyn."

"Oh, hi, Mr. and Mrs. Wakefield." She shook hands with a neighbor and his wife.

"You remember Sherry, our daughter?"

"Yes, of course." She smiled at the tall blonde, but the smile was not returned. "And I'm sure you remember my sister Skylar."

"Oh, yes," Mr. Wakefield replied. "I'm always struck at how different Dane's daughters look."

"Yes." Caitlyn's heart squeezed. "Dad said he marked us with his blue eyes so that he'd know we were his."

Mrs. Wakefield glanced toward her grandmother. "How is Dorie?"

"She's coping." Cait didn't want to discuss Gran in a room full of people. "If you'll excuse us, we were going to the buffet table."

"Oh, yes, yes." Mr. Wakefield waved them away.

"That blonde was glaring at you," Sky whispered.

"Yeah. She thought Judd should have proposed to her instead of me."

"Well, the nerve."

They reached the buffet. There was prime rib, shrimp on ice and everything in between. Cait reached for two plates, one for Gran and one for her.

Sky filled Maddie's and her own.

"Maddie trusts you to choose for her?"

"She eats like a bird and I'm stuffing everything imaginable on here."

Plates full, the sisters headed to their table.

"Why haven't Judd and the blonde hooked up since then?" Sky asked.

"I don't know and I don't care."

"Caitlyn?"

She turned to Joe Bob Shoemaker, a rancher who bought hay from her.

"Is that you?" He eyed her up and down, clutching a drink in his hand. "Hot damn, I didn't know you had some of those things." He gestured with his glass at her breasts.

She sighed. "Yeah, every woman comes equipped with boobs. It's pretty much standard."

"And, damn, you got legs, too. Never see 'em in those jeans and boots you wear."

"Is there a problem?" Walker, the constable and only law in High Cotton, strolled over. An ex-marine, he was big and impressive. Everyone called him Walker. Most people didn't know his first name, and those who did never used it.

"Just Joe Bob being an ass," Cait replied.

"Ooh, I'm wounded." Joe Bob clutched his chest.

"Excuse my husband." Charlene, his wife, came up behind him. "Go get some food or I'm leaving."

Joe Bob saluted with the glass.

Charlene yanked it out of his hand and pointed to the buffet. "Food."

The rancher stomped off, muttering, "Damn wife. Free booze and she won't let me drink."

"I'm sorry, Cait," Charlene exclaimed. "Liquor short-circuits his manners."

"Don't worry about it."

"You look gorgeous in that dress."

"Thank you. Nice seeing you, Charlene." Cait held up the plates. "We better go. Our food is getting cold."

"See you later."

Maddie rushed forward to help with the plates, and since Walker still stood there, Cait felt she should introduce them.

"This is Walker, our constable, and Walker, these are my sisters, Madison and Skylar."

"Nice to finally meet y'all. I do remember seeing y'all at the funeral, but I was on duty and didn't get a chance to visit." As they shook hands, he said to Maddie, "Ma'am, I must say you look as young as my daughter."

"How old is she?" Maddie asked in her polite manner.

"Ten."

"Ten!"

Unflappable, understanding Maddie glared at him, and Cait knew her sister was about to lose her cool. "Bye, Walker." She shuffled Maddie toward their table.

"He said I looked like a ten-year-old. The nerve of him!"

"He was just being nice." Cait brushed it off.

"Yeah, and he's not bad looking," Sky quipped.

They shared a chuckle as they joined their grandmother.

"Here you go, Gran." Cait placed her plate in front of her. "Prime rib, shrimp, roasted potatoes with parsley and grilled asparagus."

"Thank you, baby."

Maddie looked aghast at her plate. "Sky, I can't eat all this."

"Just try."

The party wore on and Cait found she kept watching the door. Where was Judd? Was he not coming?

What did she care?

Once Gran grew tired, they were leaving. It couldn't be soon enough for her.

JUDD SAT AT HIS DESK in his bedroom, going over the feed ledger and inputting information into his laptop. He heard faint noises from downstairs, but ignored them.

He wasn't planning on making an appearance.

His door swung open and his mother stood there. My God, she did look like a fairy godmother in that cloud of gold. She glanced at his tux, still in the plastic from the cleaners, on his bed.

"Not coming to the party?"

"Nope."

She walked in, her long skirt rustling like feathers against tinfoil.

"Everyone in High Cotton is here, and some of our friends from Austin. Janna Durham came especially to see you."

"I didn't invite her." He turned back to his laptop. Janna was one of those women who tried her best to get him to the altar. She never understood that he wasn't interested in marriage. He didn't relish another foray into that minefield. Caitlyn had broken him of the marriage bug. He'd rather stay single.

"And the Belles made it."

He didn't respond.

"Madison and Skylar are lovely, but Caitlyn is causing quite a stir in a red strapless dress. Every man in the room finds he can't take his eyes off her. The band is fixing to start playing, and she'll be dancing the rest of the night. Enjoy your solitude."

"If that's your subtle way of getting me downstairs, you're out of luck. I don't care what Caitlyn's wearing or not wearing."

In his mind's eye he saw her at the windmill with sweat and mud trickling down her cleavage. It irritated him that he remembered that so vividly.

"My dear son, I would never pressure you to do anything. I'm not your father."

He turned to frown at her. "What are you talking about?"

"Jack pressured you to marry Caitlyn."

He slammed the laptop shut and stood. "Dad didn't force me to do anything I didn't want to."

"Does Caitlyn know that?"

"It doesn't matter." His voice rose as he talked. "It happened fourteen years ago and it's over. Done. Kaput. Do you understand?"

"Good." She walked to him and slipped her arm through his. He stiffened; he couldn't help it. His reaction was a reflex from years of pretending she didn't exist. Much the same feeling he had for Caitlyn. "There are so many beautiful young women downstairs just waiting for you to make their night. I'd hate to think that Caitlyn has you hiding up here in your room."

"Caitlyn has no control over me, and I told you from the start I wasn't taking part in this fiasco."

"Tut-tut." Renee tapped his nose with an artificial, manicured nail. "You seem rather defensive."

"Go to your party," he said through clenched teeth, "and leave me the hell alone."

"Whatever you say, dear son." She swished out the door in a cloud of gold.

He sat on his bed and the party noise vibrated around him. Something his mother had said stuck with him. Did people think he was hiding? And when had he ever cared what people thought?

But it still stung.

He jumped up. He was getting out of the house and away from the party. At the door, he stared back at the tux on his bed.

Was he running?

THE BALL WAS in full swing and the band was revving up to something lively. Some of the tables had been removed to make room for people to dance.

Caitlyn thought this would be a good time to leave. She leaned over and whispered to her grandmother. "Gran, are you ready to go home?"

"Where are your manners? We can't leave in the middle of a party. It's just not done."

Yes, heaven forbid.

"Here comes a waiter," Sky said. "Let's have some champagne."

"And lots of it." Cait reached for a glass.

Renee appeared in the doorway and a hush fell over the crowd. "I would like to thank everyone for coming tonight and—"

"My mother and I would like to thank you." Suddenly Judd was there, and contrary to every sane thought in her head, Cait couldn't look away. Not from his handsome face. And not from the years that stretched behind her like a path covered with thorns. Painful. And littered with what-could-have-beens.

His tux fit like a movie star's across broad shoulders and that long, muscled body. Expensive cowboy boots covered his feet—only in Texas could you wear boots with a tuxedo, but it suited the man as he gave a perfunctory smile to his guests.

He was a rancher with money and power, and it showed in every chiseled Clint Eastwood-like feature on his face. It showed in the way he moved and in the way he spoke. He was a man to be reckoned with. A man only a fool would cross.

Cait moved uneasily and realized she was spilling champagne into her cleavage. Good grief.

She grabbed a napkin and dabbed, under several men's watchful eyes.

Old fools!

A Texas waltz played, and Renee and Judd took to the floor, dancing round and round. And the night dragged on. Judd danced with every woman in the room, including Gran, Maddie and Sky. Not once did he look in Cait's direction. Not once did he ask her to dance.

That was fine with her. She had plenty of partners. And she didn't *want* to dance with him. It was better if he didn't touch her. Southern manners only went so far.

She escaped to the powder room and turned on the gold faucets. Patting her face with a tissue, she soaked up the coolness and stared at the ornate wood trim, the crimson and soft pink walls. A fresh bouquet of pink irises graced the vanity, as did monogrammed towels and soaps. Everything was elegant. Everything was Renee.

Cait yanked opened the door and ran into Brenda Sue. Someone up there was testing her patience.

"Wow, Caitlyn, where did you get that dress? I want one just like it. I never knew you had it in you to wear something like that. You know, you never did in high school. But tonight you're showing actual cleavage. I'm surprised your grandmother allowed it. She's like, you know, rather high on morals and manners and things I've never heard about. Is anyone in the bathroom? I really have to pee. But I don't want to miss any of the action." She knocked on the door without taking a breath. "I'll just use one of the other bathrooms. You know I have the run of the place and…"

Caitlyn walked off down the hall and didn't look back. She made her way through the dancing couples to the veranda. Japanese lanterns lit up the trees with a magical glow. In a dark corner, she sat down and took a deep breath. It was quieter out here. Couples swayed together and the night air was warm yet soothing.

Feeling a chill, she ran her hands up her arms. She lifted her eyes and saw Judd standing in the shadows a few feet away. Her eyes locked with his and her heart thudded with the force of a nine pound hammer.

Her first thought was to walk away, but this time pride wouldn't let her. This time she was standing her ground and facing Judd.

CHAPTER TWELVE

"EVERYONE IS EXPECTING US to dance," Judd said in a voice that flowed around her like a warm blanket and wrapped her in memories.

The good ones.

"Yes," she managed to reply.

He held out his hand.

Go to hell. Not in this lifetime ever again. When hell freezes over. The comebacks were right there in her throat. All she had to do was say the words and walk away from him. She could do that. She'd done it before.

Something stronger than her pride moved her forward. She placed her hand in his and he pulled her into his arms. Her soft curves pressed into the hardness of his body and they began to move to "Bluest Eyes in Texas." Her forehead rested against his jaw and his sandalwood scent shot her estrogen levels up a few notches. The tautness of his muscles shot her levels through the roof. But she didn't pull away. She was on autopilot.

Still dancing, they moved out of the shadows and among the other couples. Out of the corner of her eye Cait saw Maddie, Sky, Gran and Renee watching them. Nothing registered but the male body pressed against hers. She had to admit she'd missed his touch. She'd missed him. That part of their relationship had been nothing less than fantastic.

Some couples stopped dancing, but Cait and Judd danced on. In his arms she felt like a princess—the belle of the ball. He pulled her closer and there was nothing left to the imagination; every muscle, every sinew, she felt. And she floated away to a happy place where fairy tales came true.

"Why wasn't this enough, Caitlyn?" His throaty voice broke through the clouds to reality.

She pulled back slightly to look into his dark eyes. It felt strange to have this conversation after fourteen years. "Because sex and love are two different things."

"They're the same to me."

"They're not to me. Sex is an act. Love is a feeling in here…." She removed her hand from his to place it over his heart. Her eyes holding his, she added, "Sex is fleeting. Love lasts forever."

He glanced down at her hand. "I didn't know I had a heart until you broke it."

Her breath felt heavy at his admission. "You could have come after me."

"You could have come back."

"But that would have changed nothing. It still would have been an arranged marriage without love." She pushed away from him then. "So go ahead and get even. Take your revenge. Hurt me if that makes you feel better. The sad part is that I've hurt myself more." She tore away from him and ran from the room, past startled guests, out the front door, down the front steps and into the night.

She lost a shoe and sank to the ground and began to laugh. Laughter turned to tears. Try as she might she couldn't stop them, so she gave up and howled.

Maddie and Sky eased down by her. She sat on the grass and wiped away tears with the back of her hand. Her sisters didn't say anything. They just hugged her, which was what she needed.

Maddie held up her red high heel. "Would Cinderella like to try on the magical shoe?"

Cait burst into laughter once more. "Most certainly. Even though I've never heard of Cinderella in a come-hither red dress. She looks virginal, like you."

"Yeah, right." Maddie ruffled her skirt. "That Walker guy had the nerve to ask me to dance. I told him my mommy doesn't allow me to."

"He's a hottie, so I danced with him." Sky

nudged Cait playfully. "I told him we only let Maddie out of the attic on special occasions, and that she's a little gun-shy or man-shy."

"Hardy har-har." Maddie made a face at Sky, then linked her arm through Cait's. "Let's go home."

"First Cait has to slip on the magical shoe."

"Hell's bells, Sky, there's no magic in it," she protested.

"I beg to differ," Maddie said, holding it out.

Cait slipped her foot in.

Nothing happened.

Same old heartache. Same old bizarre evening.

"Okay." Maddie wrinkled her nose. "Maybe there isn't any such thing as a fairy tale."

"You got it. Let's load up the Lincoln, pick up Gran and get the hell out of Dodge."

"Good plan," Sky murmured as they got to their feet. "I guess y'all know we're going to have grass stains on these dresses."

"So? After tonight we'll retire the dresses from hell." Cait peered through the darkness at the sea of cars. "Now where is that old Lincoln?"

"Whistle, Cait, like you always do," Maddie suggested. "Maybe that guy who was ogling you will come running."

She put her fingers to her mouth and blew. Nothing happened. They burst into a fit of giggles. "We've had too much champagne," Cait said.

"May I help you?" The young man appeared abruptly, scaring the living daylights out of them.

"Yes. We'd like our car, please. The Lincoln," Cait told him, trying not to snicker.

"The old one?"

"Yes. The old one."

"I'll bring it around."

The Lincoln rolled to a stop in front of them.

"I'm driving," Sky said, and rounded the car.

Cait slid into the passenger's seat and Maddie climbed in the back. "Make a circle so we can pick up Gran," Cait instructed.

"Yes, bossy."

She shot her the finger.

Sky zoomed forward and came to a screeching stop at the front door. Maddie jumped out to assist Gran, who was waiting on the veranda with their hostess.

Gran got in, and Renee waved. Cait did not wave back. Sky tore out of the driveway.

"We're going home, Gran," Sky said, glancing in the rearview mirror.

"Yes, my baby, we're going home." There was a long pause and then Gran asked, "Caitlyn, baby, are you okay?"

"Yes, I'm fine."

"Did Judd hurt your feelings?"

Her gut tightened. "Naw. He just bruised my pride. I'm tough."

"Women shouldn't be tough, Caitlyn." Her tone suggested Cait should mind her p's and q's.

"Come on, Gran," Sky said, negotiating a turn. "Belles are tough. We all are."

"That's why you don't have husbands."

"And that's the name of that tune," Cait whispered to Sky.

They rode in silence for a moment.

"It was a lovely party," Gran said. "I kept waiting for your father to show up."

Cait and Sky exchanged a glance.

"Before any of you say it, I know Dane is dead."

"Yes," Cait replied. And added a private *thank God* for not having to say the words.

THEY WALKED Gran into the house and up to her bedroom. But Cait wasn't ready to close her eyes. Her engine was still running. While Maddie and Sky helped Gran, she went down to the parlor and to her father's wine collection. She pulled out a merlot and uncorked it. Breathing the fragrant scent, she closed her eyes. *Oh, yeah.* This was what she needed. Tipping up the bottle, she walked to the kitchen. She chugalugged right out the door and all the way to the barn.

Within minutes she had a bridle on Jaz. From

the refrigerator in the barn, she grabbed two carrots and stuffed them into her cleavage. Then she hitched up her red skirt and slid on bareback, the bottle in one hand. One high heel fell to the ground and she left it there.

She had something she wanted to do, and she rode like hell through the night.

JUDD SAT IN HIS STUDY with a bottle of bourbon and a shot glass in front of him. He should have never gone down to the party. But God, she was beautiful. That red dress was something out of his fantasies. Every man in the room, married or single, had wanted her. He was no exception.

The dancing part was great. Conversing always brought trouble, though. They'd never connected on that level, and it was important to her. Why did women always want to talk and analyze everything to death?

He was an action man and he didn't like any of that intense inner emotional crap. That's why he was sitting here drinking bourbon—alone. Tyra or Jenna would be happy to keep him company, and he wouldn't have to do a lot of conversing, either. Still, he'd left the party soon after Caitlyn. She pretty much put the lid on the night.

For fourteen years they'd managed to stay apart, and in a matter of a few days they were smack-dab in the middle of each other's lives. He wanted her to bend. He wanted her to beg.

And he was going to grow into a lonely old man waiting for that to happen. He threw the shot glass at the wall and it exploded in a burst of amber liquid.

As he watched bourbon trail down the paneling, his cell phone buzzed. It was 2:00 a.m. Who was calling this late? He picked the device up and saw it was Harland. Something had to be wrong.

He clicked on. "Yes."

"Sorry to bother you so late, but we have a situation at the stables."

He stood and ran a hand through his already tousled hair. "What is it?"

"You need to see for yourself."

"I'll be right there." Judd still wore his tux trousers and his white shirt hung loose over them. He didn't bother to change.

Harland met him at the stables. "I heard a noise so I thought I'd check on the new horse. I'll show you what I found."

Judd followed him to Whiskey Red's stall. They'd put blinders on the horse and she'd settled down. The blinders were now off and Caitlyn sat on the floor of the enclosure, her back against a wall, sipping from a bottle of wine. A carrot poked out of her cleavage. She still wore the red dress and the skirt was bunched between her bare thighs. She was barefooted. Disheveled black hair cascaded around her shoulders.

A familiar longing tightened his lower abdomen.

"Hey, Judd." She raised the bottle.

"I'll take care of this," he told Harland.

"I tried to pull her out of there, but the horse gets riled, so I left her alone."

"Thanks." Judd leaned on the stall door. "What are you doing, Caitlyn?"

"Visiting the horse you took from me."

"Looks to me like you're drinking."

"Yep. That, too." She tipped up the bottle.

"Get out of the stall."

She squinted at him. "Nope. Don't think so."

"You're trespassing."

"Yep. I am."

She was sloshed and he didn't want to hurt her by dragging her out. The thought hit him like the bourbon deep in his belly—warm, fuzzy and jolting. Everything he'd done recently had been meant to hurt her. Maybe that hadn't been his intention at all. Maybe all he wanted was her attention.

A sobering thought.

"Come out of the stall, Caitlyn. It's late."

She lifted the bottle. "Make me."

He slid the latch of the stall door open and stepped in. Red immediately threw up her head, fidgeting in an agitated manner.

Judd fully intended to make Caitlyn leave the stall, but once he saw the pain in her eyes, that plan went south. Instead he sank down beside her in the dirt and straw.

She handed him the bottle. "Want a drink?"

"No, thank you."

She took a swig and then peered into the bottle with one eye. "Damn, it's all gone. Someone drank my wine."

"You did."

"No, no, no." She shook her head. "You did. You took my royalties, my horse and—"

"I bought your royalties and your horse. They weren't cheap, either."

"Why? Why did you have to do that?" Her blurred blue eyes tried to focus on him.

"You're drunk," was all he could say.

"Yep." She jammed the bottle into the hay. "And it never felt so damn good." She plucked the carrot from her cleavage. "Here, Red, have a carrot before I have to leave Mr. High-and-Mighty's stables."

The horse munched on the offering and Cait rested her head against the wall. For a moment he thought she was out, but she wasn't. She was close, though.

The overhead light cast shadows across them. The scents of manure, horse, sweet feed and hay radiated through the barn. A horse neighed and another stomped in its stall. All normal scents and sounds, but nothing was normal about this night.

"You didn't have to run away tonight."

"Yes, I did." Cait hiccuped.

"Why?"

"Oh, please." She staggered to her feet. "Your goal in life now is to hurt me. Well—" she clutched at the stall wall for support "—you've succeeded, but you'll never get High Five. Ooh." She grabbed her head. "The stall is moving."

He rose to his feet, not bothering to dust off his clothes. "Why do you keep fighting this? It's just a matter of time."

"Don't... Don't—" she jabbed a finger at him "—say that...." She swayed like a felled tree and he caught her before she crumpled to the ground. He swung her over his shoulder and left the stall, latching the gate behind him.

"Put me down," she yelled, beating on his back.

He kept walking toward his Ford Lariat truck, parked at the garages.

"The shoe had no magic. Poof. It didn't work."

He didn't know what the hell she was talking about. Yanking open the door, he deposited her on the passenger side. He waited to see if she'd try to get out, but she didn't. Her head dropped onto the leather headrest, her tousled black hair a striking sight against the red dress.

"If you'd been a prince, the shoe would have been magical," she muttered. "But you're no prince." She turned toward him, her eyes managing to hold his. "You're the devil."

He closed the door and a chill shot up his spine. Walking around to the driver's side, he said to hell with her. He didn't care what she thought of him. His conscience, something he hadn't been in contact with for some time, chose that moment to awaken and mock him.

From the moment Dane had offered him the royalties, Judd had felt a burst of energy. He would now have his revenge. He would make her hurt the way she had hurt him. But ironically, hurting Caitlyn was harder than he'd ever expected.

CHAPTER THIRTEEN

JUDD TURNED THE KEY and the engine hummed to life.

"My horse. I can ride my horse," Caitlyn muttered as the truck moved onto the road.

"Where is your horse?"

"I tied her to a tree by the barn…I think."

"I'll return her tomorrow."

"I don't need…your help." Her voice was growing weak and sleepy.

He didn't say anything else, just drove toward High Five. No other vehicles were on the road at this time of the morning, so he made the trip in record time. He pulled to a stop in front of the Belle house. The front porch light was shining brightly and a light was on at the barn.

He touched her arm. "You're home."

She sat up straight and grabbed her head. "Geez, Louise." She opened one eye to peer through the darkness. "How did I get here?"

"Guess." His gaze held hers. "You were too drunk to ride a horse."

"Listen…" She winced.

"Get out of the truck. You're home."

Caitlyn stared at him though the darkness. His tousled hair falling across his forehead and his dark growth of beard evoked so many memories. Good memories of when she'd thought he loved her.

Without thinking clearly, she slid a hand around his neck, caressed his roughened skin and pulled his face toward hers. She touched his lips gently, almost reverently. It took a split second for remembered emotions to explode.

He took over the kiss, cupping her face with both hands, and time floated away, as did the years, as they found comfort in a kiss that bound them together. Tongues and lips knew the drill. Memories like this weren't forgotten, just buried beneath the pain.

He tasted of bourbon, and the heady sensation was making her drunk all over again. Or was it just Judd?

He was the first to draw back. "Why did you do that?" His voice vibrated as smoothly as the engine of his fancy truck.

She licked her lips. "To see if my collection of memories is gold plated or the real thing?"

"And?"

Cait would never know what her response would have been because Cooper tapped on the window, and when she glanced up she saw Maddie and Sky hurrying down the sidewalk.

Cait smiled slyly. "You'll never know." She opened the door and almost fell out.

"Everything okay?" Coop asked as he caught her.

"Yep," she replied, staggering. Coop steadied her. "I'm a little drunk, though."

"Cait," Sky called. "Where have you been?"

She glanced at Judd and wasn't sure how to answer that. It had been a bizarre evening. What had possessed her to kiss him? She blamed it on the liquor, and closed the door. She didn't want to see Judd's face any longer. It made her weak.

The truck pulled out of the driveway and Sky and Maddie rushed to her. "Where have you been?" Sky demanded.

"*Are* you okay?" Coop asked, and Sky shot him a this-is-none-of-your-business look.

"Yes, Coop, thanks." Cait smiled at him to ease any hard feelings. "I got a little sidetracked tonight."

"I saw Jaz was gone and I was worried."

"I took a midnight ride to visit Red."

"You didn't." Sky was aghast.

"Yes, I did, and I got caught." She picked up her filthy skirt. "Now I'm going inside to crash. Night, Coop."

"Night." He strolled back to the bunkhouse.

Maddie and Sky linked their arms through hers and they marched together toward the house, through the door and up the stairs.

"Your dress is ruined," Maddie said, inspecting Cait in the light.

"That's what happens when you wallow in the stables with a bottle of wine."

"Sometimes you're like a loose cannon." Sky opened the bathroom door. "And you stink."

"Shit happens, I suppose," she replied, stepping inside and closing the door on her sisters.

She turned on the bathtub taps, stripped out of the ridiculous dress and sank into the warm water. It felt heavenly, and wonderful to wash away the grime. Washing away the memories was something else entirely. Not a task that could be done with mere soap and water.

Why had she kissed him? Why? Her hand went to her lips and she still felt Judd's soft caress, so different from the strong and powerful man that he was. Liquored up, she couldn't resist or deny the pull she always experienced when she was around him. That was her only explanation. And it didn't change a thing in her life.

He was still the enemy.

She quickly got out of the tub, dried off and slipped on a big T-shirt. Opening the door, she found her sisters standing there with their old sleeping bags.

"We're camping on the veranda tonight, or what's left of the night," Maddie told her. "It might be a long time before we see each other again."

"I'm game." Cait picked up her bag and they trudged out to the porch and got comfy.

"Gran asleep?" she asked, rolling out her bedding between Maddie's and Sky's.

"Yes. The dancing wore her out." Maddie wiggled on top of her bag. It was too warm to slide inside.

There was silence for a moment as they absorbed the warmth and peace of the night.

"What were you and Judd talking about?" Sky asked. "We were looking for you and saw the truck drive up. What took you so long to get out?"

"I was making a fool of myself." She folded her hands behind her head. "Yep. I'm getting good at that."

Sky rose up on an elbow. "What happened?"

"Well, remember I was highly intoxicated…."

"Anyone who would visit a horse in the dead of night has to be intoxicated or insane. Should we take a vote?"

"Shut up, Sky," she said, and moved uneasily.

"So what happened?" Sky pressed.

She didn't answer for a moment. "I just wanted

to make sure Red was comfortable. She's very temperamental. I took her a treat, a couple of carrots, and I took a treat for myself—a bottle of wine."

"After all the champagne we consumed!"

"Yes, Betty Crocker, it wasn't a brilliant idea, and my head is pounding. Let's go to sleep."

"Not until you tell us what you and Judd were talking about." Sky wouldn't give up.

"Geez, you're relentless. It was the same old, same old." She moved uneasily again as the truth weaved its way around her heart. "I sat there looking at him through liquored up eyes, but all I could see and feel was the way I used to love him." She watched the moon hanging in the sky like a neon sign, and was sure the fictional man in the moon had a come-on-in sign stapled on his chest. It was that warm. That inviting. Breaking down her barriers. "So I kissed him."

Maddie sat up straight. "You did what?"

"Well, well." Sky rose also, sitting cross-legged. "Now what does that say?"

"It says I was drunk out of my mind."

"It says you still love him," Maddie countered.

Cait sat up and wrapped her arms around her bare legs. "Maybe. Maybe I'll always love him, but that doesn't change a thing. Judd hasn't altered. He's still like his father, needing to have power over a woman because he feels she's less than he is. I can't live with a man who thinks that way. I can't love him, either."

"So, what? You're going to sneak over at night and have sex with him, and during the day you're still enemies?"

"Sky, I didn't have sex with him."

"I'm sticking to my original suggestions," she stated. "As a woman, you have the power to make him beg. Use everything in your arsenal, and High Five and Southern Cross will be yours. Think of it as a contest and the big prize is Judd."

"Judd is not a prize and I don't have an arsenal."

"Well, honey, you should have seen yourself tonight. Judd couldn't take his eyes off you, and when you danced there was not a smidgen of daylight between you."

"Sky…"

"Can we please talk about something else?" Maddie asked. "We only have a few more hours together. Let's don't spend it bickering."

"Okay," Cait said with a smug expression. "Let's talk about Kira. When are you going to tell Gran?"

"When I see fit."

"Gran has a right to see her great-granddaughter."

"I feel awful lying to her, but I have little choice. I've been trying to get in touch with Todd so he can get his parents off my back, but so far no response. Until that happens I have to stay in hiding."

Sky stretched out on her sleeping bag and Cait and Maddie followed suit. They were quiet as crickets serenaded. A horse neighed and a dog barked in response to a coyote howling in the distance. The sounds of High Five. The ranch that Cait loved, but how long would she be allowed to stay here?

As if reading her thoughts, Sky asked, "Do you think you can show a profit in six months?"

"I'm going to give it my best shot."

"But you have no help," Maddie pointed out.

"That's why I work fourteen-hour days."

"The simple solution is just to sell," Sky said. "Gran can still live here, and I'm sure if you ask nicely, Judd will let you stay, too."

"I don't do *asking nicely* to Judd Calhoun." The mere thought made her stomach roll.

"Leave Cait alone," Maddie stated. "We agreed to six months, and she even sold Red, so stop browbeating her."

There was silence for a moment and then Sky said, "Okay. I'm in for the long haul."

They gave each other the customary high five and snuggled onto their bags, settling down for the rest of the night. But Cait stayed awake long after she heard her sisters' wispy snoring. Tomorrow she would be alone again with Gran, and fighting to save High Five.

Somewhere between lucidness and sleep she

wondered if she was fighting a losing battle. In the end, she could lose it all. But she still had to take that risk.

JUDD WALKED INTO THE BARN to check on Whiskey Red. She raised her head with a nervous neigh.

"It's okay, girl." He tried to reassure her, and she seemed to settle down. He saw the wine bottle and opened the stall door to retrieve it. The thoroughbred watched him, but stayed calm. Along the wall, Judd glimpsed a flash of red. He picked up a red high heel. He hadn't noticed it before. It must have been behind Caitlyn.

On his way out he flipped off the lights and tossed the wine bottle into the trash. He glanced at the shoe and started to trash it, too, then stopped.

Caitlyn had said something about the shoe having no magic. That if he was a prince, it would have been magical. Was she talking about a stupid fairy tale? No, she was too mature for that. But it was romantic stuff. Stuff that was important to her.

He strolled to the house with the shoe in his hand. The place was in darkness and endless quiet prevailed—the way he liked it. His study light was on and he headed there for the bourbon.

Placing the shoe in the center of his desk, he poured himself a shot and sank into his chair with a groan. What a night!

He licked his lips, still tasting the wine on Caitlyn's. Magic was there. Why couldn't she see it? Why couldn't she feel it? He downed the amber liquid in the shot glass and gazed at the shoe.

It seemed to taunt him.

The shoe wasn't magical.

Did she honestly think she could slip her foot into a magic shoe and he would love her? He had never loved her, had he? He desired her. He wanted her. Those were the emotions he understood.

Oh, God. He jammed his hands through his hair and then poured himself another drink. Everything was supposed to be simple. With the royalties gone, Caitlyn's only option would be to sell High Five. Even though she wouldn't want to, her sisters would force her hand. He'd have his revenge and she would disappear out of his life forever. He wouldn't see her in High Cotton. He wouldn't see her anywhere.

His mother had warned him that Caitlyn would come back fighting. She'd been right. Now Caitlyn was making his life a living hell.

He downed the bourbon. She was making him aware of how much he wanted her. That was lust, not love. And there was no magic in that.

After opening a drawer, he reached for the shoe and flung it inside.

So much for magic.

And Caitlyn Belle.

CHAPTER FOURTEEN

THE NEXT MORNING SAW a tearful goodbye. After a big breakfast, Etta drove Maddie and Sky to the airport. Gran went along so she could spend more time with her granddaughters.

Cait didn't have time to be nostalgic. There was work waiting for her. She met Coop and Rufus at the barn.

"The baler broke, but Ru and I got it fixed last night," Coop told her. "We're ready to go."

"God willing and the baler doesn't break again, we should be through by the end of June." Ru climbed into his truck. "There's still a lot of hay on the ground, though."

"I'll check the herds and then give y'all a hand," Cait called.

Coop jumped onto the tractor connected to the baler. "Jaz was in the corral this morning. And I found a red high heel in the barn. Don't know where it came from and I'm not asking. I put it on a shelf. See you later," he added, with a twinkle in his eye.

She waved as they rolled out of sight, and then glanced toward the corral. There was Jaz, and her bridle was hanging on the fence. Had Judd brought back the horse or had he sent one of the cowhands? Either way, she just wanted to forget the miserable evening. Her aching head made that a little hard, though—a reminder that was going to be with her for the rest of the day.

Saddling up, Cait found her eyes straying to the red shoe laid haphazardly on a shelf. She had no idea where its mate was. The only explanation was that she'd lost it on the way to Southern Cross, and she'd just as soon forget about that visit.

She headed for the pastures. Water was flowing in all of them, the windmill spinning like a large whirling fan. The stock tanks were getting lower, though. Local ranchers needed rain badly.

In the last pasture, she didn't see Boss, and worried he might be on the Southern Cross again. Cait rode through the herd twice and still didn't spot him. Damn! Then she saw him coming out of the woods, looking a little scuffed up. He'd probably been fighting with the other bulls, which was his modus operandi. But she was relieved he wasn't trying to court the Southern Cross cows again.

At midday she headed back to the ranch house, and was surprised to find Etta and Gran weren't back. Cait checked for messages on the phone and there weren't any. If something was wrong, there would have been a message, so she told herself not to worry.

She made sandwiches and packed a lunch to carry to Coop and Rufus. Afterward, she worked the tractor with the front fork to lift the round bales from the field and place them along the fence. It was a hot, scorching day—the type of weather to be indoors with air-conditioning or in a swimming pool.

But she wasn't an indoor person, and lying around a pool wasn't her, either. She must enjoy cruel and inhuman punishment, Cait decided ruefully. Sweat rolled down her back and soaked the waistband of her jeans. It coated her whole body, and the warm breeze made her feel as if she was in a sauna.

She lowered a round bale to the ground and massaged the calluses on her hands. *This isn't women's work.* How many times had her father said that to her? And how many times had she tried to prove him wrong?

Was she trying to hold on to High Five for Gran, or trying to prove something to her father? As she removed her hat and wiped sweat from her brow, she thought she might be proving him right.

He'd always said that a woman's place was in the home, making babies and pleasing her husband. None of his daughters had cottoned to the idea, so to speak, but he'd never wavered in his conviction. And neither had Caitlyn.

As the sun sank in the west, Cait suspected she was going to grow old clinging to her beliefs. Nothing would ever change her mind.

Not even Judd Calhoun.

Or her love for him.

That thought stayed with her as they made their way home.

She came to an abrupt stop in the kitchen doorway. Etta was at the stove, and Maddie and Gran were setting the table.

"Maddie, I thought you left." She removed her hat and placed it on a rack.

Her sister wiped her hands on her apron. "I thought about it all the way into town. I now have the cash to pay off my debts, so I stopped and called my mom and wired her the money. She's going to pay the bills and I can stay here and help you. You need it."

"Maddie…"

"Belles stand and fight. Isn't that one of Dad's sayings? And I have a stake in this ranch, too."

"Oh, Maddie!" They hugged tightly.

"Why are you girls talking about such things?" Gran asked, straightening a napkin. "Your father takes care of all that."

Cait and Maddie glanced at each other and knew a response would be useless.

"Here, Gran." Maddie pulled out a chair. "Have a seat. Etta's chicken fried steak is almost ready."

Gran sat as Cooper and Rufus walked through the door.

When Coop spied Maddie, he took a step backward. "Oh, I didn't know we still had company." Before he could take another step, Maddie grabbed his arm.

"No, you don't, Cooper Yates. I don't bite. I promise."

Maddie's sweet smile thawed the cowboy faster than the Texas heat. "I just don't want to intrude."

"You're not," Cait said. "And I'm starving. How about you?"

After supper, Maddie helped Etta with the dishes.

"See you at home, Etta." Rufus shuffled out the door and Cooper followed.

The phone rang and Cait ran to answer it.

"This is Gil Bardwell. I'm trying to locate Caitlyn Belle."

"This is Caitlyn."

"Chance Hardin gave me your number. I'm the foreman of a large road construction company and I need sand and gravel. Chance said you have some to sell."

"Yes. Yes, I do." She took a long breath. This

was too good to be true, but she wasn't looking this gift horse in the mouth. They arranged to meet in the morning and discuss a price.

"Was that Sky?" Maddie asked from the doorway.

"No." Cait hugged her. "You're bringing me good luck. That was a man who wants to buy sand and gravel. It's going to help tremendously. I have to make some calls to check on prices." She picked up the phone and glanced at Maddie. "Could you please help Gran? I'll be up as soon as I finish."

"Don't worry about Gran. We're going to watch an old movie. *Giant,* with Elizabeth Taylor and Rock Hudson."

"Thanks. I'll try to catch the end."

By ten o'clock Cait's eyes wouldn't stay open any longer, so she trudged upstairs. But she had numbers and knew what prices to ask. There was a light beaming at the end of the tunnel of her nightmare.

Gran was sound asleep with Maddie curled up at her side, a popcorn bowl in the crook of her arm. Cait clicked off the TV and shook her sister.

"Time for bed," she whispered.

Maddie sat up, stretching. "I didn't realize I was so tired."

"Me, neither," Cait admitted. "See you in the morning." At the door she looked back. "Thank you."

"That's what sisters are for."

"I'm sorry I was on the phone so long. Sky couldn't call."

"I phoned her on my cell. I told her you were making big deals. She made it home safely and said she can't stop holding Kira." Maddie kissed her cheek. "'Night, sis."

Cait showered and fell into a dead sleep, but right before the hazy, blissful slumber claimed her she saw Judd's face and heard his words.

Why wasn't this enough?

THE NEXT MORNING was hectic as everyone hurried to work. After breakfast Coop and Rufus went to the hay field and Cait rushed to meet Mr. Bardwell. Within an hour, they had hammered out a deal. He explained they would have to dig forty feet deep or more with a dragline excavator, creating some steep hills and deep valleys. He promised to level the land as much as he could and keep damages to a minimum.

She showed him the places on the ranch he could dig, the areas Grandfather Bart had sold from years ago. The pastures with the cattle were off-limits.

Maddie stayed at the house with Gran, and that arrangement worked well. Cait didn't worry about Gran with her sister there.

Maddie had also undertaken the job of cleaning the house from top to bottom. Dust didn't have a chance with her around. And most days she brought lunch to the fields so they didn't have to make the trip to the house.

Several people had called about buying hay, and Cait sold what they didn't need. The ranch was taking a turn for the better. If her luck held, she'd have the books in the black before the six-month time period. She couldn't let up, though. Every day she had to stay on top of things.

It was time to tag the new baby calves and round up the older ones to sell. Maddie saddled up to help. She was a good rider; their father had seen to that. The job was dusty, hot and tedious, but Maggie never faltered.

With the help of the dogs, they herded the cattle from the pastures into the corral. There, Cait and Coop dismounted and waded into the herd. He caught a baby calf and she marked it, using an ear tag gun. More than once Cait stepped in cow crap, and the scent filled her nostrils. She never stopped, though. They continued until every baby was tagged with the number of its mother.

Then they saddled up again and separated the herd, cutting out mothers and babies into another corral. Rufus worked the gate and Maddie helped; the dogs nipped at the cows' feet. Cows bellowed and the dust was suffocating. Finally, only the older calves were left in the corral. Rufus and Maddie herded the other animals back to the pastures.

"I'll load 'em up later and get 'em to the auction barn for tomorrow's sale," Coop said.

"Good. I'll make sure the cows are settling down." Cait glanced up as she heard riders, knowing it was too soon for Maddie and Rufus to return.

Harland and four Southern Cross cowboys rode into view.

"Uh-oh, I sense trouble." Coop wiped the sweat from his forehead with the sleeve of his chambray shirt.

Harland galloped forward. "Miss Belle, we have a problem with your bull again. I have orders not to shoot him, so you'd better come take care of the situation."

"I'll be right there." She put her foot in the stirrup and swung into the saddle. Coop did the same.

"Yates doesn't come onto Southern Cross property." Harland spit chewing tobacco onto the ground.

Cait rode out of the corral to within a foot of Harland. "Cooper goes where I go." Her voice was sharp enough to cut through a T-bone steak.

"Well, Miss Belle." Harland leaned back in the saddle. "You just might need a man to help you with this problem, so I'll allow it this time."

A round of snickers echoed from the cowboys. "Just show me where my bull is."

"Yes, ma'am." Harland jerked his bridle and shot away, the cowboys behind him. She and Cooper immediately followed. It was clear the foreman was trying to lose them, or to prove that they couldn't keep up. But she knew every inch of High Five and there was no way she'd fall behind.

They came to a gap and one of the cowboys opened it. It was farther along the fence that Boss had broken through earlier. She wondered why they weren't riding through a broken fence instead of the gap.

She pulled up as Harland and his boys stopped. All eyes were on her. Boss stood alone in the woods, with his head hanging low. He hadn't budged as the riders approached.

Cait dismounted and walked to the animal, Harland and Cooper behind her. She stood in shock for a moment at the sight in front of her. The lower part of Boss's belly was swollen and his split penis was almost hanging to the ground. Blood and pus oozed out of it. Her stomach churned with a sick feeling, but she tried to hide her reaction.

"How did this happen?" she managed to ask.

"Well, Ms. Belle, it seems your bull has taken to jumping the fence. This time he was ready for action, if you know what I mean, and he caught his main feature on the barbed wire, splitting it open. He's useless now. He has to be put down."

A low, guttural sound left Boss's throat. He was in pain and probably had an infection and fever.

"I'm not sure your boy Yates here is allowed to use a gun—being on probation and all. Looks like you'll have to do the honors."

The cowboys snickered again.

Out of the corner of her eye Cait saw Judd's black horse, and a few seconds later he was standing beside them.

"What's going on here?"

Harland relayed his story and Judd squatted to look at Boss. "Damn. He has to be put down. He's in a lot of pain."

"That's what I was telling Miss Belle."

"She won't do it," she heard a cowboy murmur.

"She hasn't got the guts," another said.

"Shut up or go back to the barn," Judd ordered.

Cait headed for her horse. "I'll do it," Coop whispered beside her.

"You'll get in trouble."

"I don't care."

"I do." She yanked her rifle from the scabbard on the saddle. She always carried one for coyotes and wild dogs that preyed on baby calves. But she'd never used it.

And she didn't know if she could use it now. The men kept watching her with smug expressions. She saw money exchange hands between two cowboys. They were betting she couldn't.

"We'll take care of the animal," Judd said.

The note in his voice that said she shouldn't have to do this ricocheted her courage into high gear. She was a woman and shouldn't be running a ranch. This was where the fictional line was drawn in the sand. She either stepped over it and did her job, or she stepped back and admitted she couldn't run this ranch.

For her, the latter was unacceptable.

"It's my animal. I'll take care of him."

"Caitlyn…"

She walked away, stopping about twenty feet from Boss. He made that gut-wrenching sound again and she knew she had to put him out of his misery.

What was the price of courage? Her pride? Her heart?

Without a second thought, she released the safety and raised the rifle. She took aim at Boss's shoulder through the crosshairs. Everything else faded away. Boss was in pain. She had to do this.

She had to do this.

The rapid beat of her heart pounded in her ears.

Her palms were sweaty, and fear like she'd never known before crawled up her spine.

She had to do this.

I'm sorry, Boss.

She squeezed the trigger. The big bull dropped with a thud. He was dead.

The rifle butt kicked her shoulder as the sound of the blast echoed across the landscape. The explosive noise caused a ringing in her ears.

She stood frozen.

After a moment she lowered the gun, walked to her horse and shoved the rifle into the scabbard. Swinging into the saddle, she said to Coop, "Get the tractor and take him back to High Five." Then she rode hell-bent for somewhere other than here.

She kept nudging Jaz on, faster and faster, her stomach churning. When she reached Crooked Creek, she jumped off and threw up until there was nothing left in her but the pain. The pain of having to kill a living thing.

On her hands and knees, she crawled some distance away and leaned against an oak tree, taking deep breaths. Her mouth tasted like bile and she wiped her hand across it. Feeling weak, she rested her head on her knees.

There was absolute quiet here in the deep woods. Just an occasional twitter of a bird, the rustling of leaves and the call of a crow. Through

the silence she heard a rider, and thought Coop
was coming to look for her.

She raised her head and saw the black horse. Judd.
The last person she wanted to see.

CHAPTER FIFTEEN

JUDD WALKED TO HER and sank into the grass. Plucking a dried sprig, he studied it as if it was a marvel of science.

She didn't speak.

Nor did he.

He lifted his eyes, and their depths were so dark she couldn't even see the pupils. "Why do you have to be so tough? You didn't have to do that."

"A man would have without a second thought, and no one would have told him not to."

"You're not a man."

"Yeah." She faked a laugh. "My father reminded me of that every day of my life. I was never the son he wanted."

"No, you're his daughter—his beautiful, brave and spirited daughter. Why does that make you less of a person?"

It was weird hearing Judd say that. It was even more weird to be sitting here talking to him. Almost as if they were the only two people in the world and he understood her and her feelings.

She took a long breath and tucked a strand of hair behind her ear. "I find it strange that you would say that. You believe every woman is beneath you, the way your father believed…and mine."

"I'm not my father." His eyes darkened to pitch-black.

"But you are. His beliefs have been ingrained into you from birth. You even told me that."

"People change."

"Yeah." *Maybe.* Judd? She doubted it. She ran a hand through the dried grass and knew they had to talk about the past. It was right there between them like a boil that needed lancing. Time to get it over with. "Let's talk about what happened."

An eyebrow darted toward the rim of his Stetson. "We've killed that already."

"No, we haven't. We've danced around the flagpole without ever saluting the flag."

"What?"

"That means we've talked about everything but the real issue—my leaving and the reason I felt the way I did."

He moved restlessly. "I thought we covered that."

"No." She drew a hot breath from the bottom of her lungs. "I didn't leave you for another man. I didn't leave you because I didn't love you. I left because you didn't support me when I learned our marriage was arranged by our fathers. You didn't support me when I wanted to return to college. I left because you didn't love me. I couldn't live with a man who doesn't put me first and treat me as his equal. I wanted it all, and I will never settle for less."

He rubbed the sprig of grass between his fingers. "I told you I'm not familiar with love. I've never had that emotion in my life."

"Bull. Even abused kids know what love is. It's a feeling inside the heart—a special feeling for one certain person. I know you have it. You just won't acknowledge it." She held up a hand. "No. You're afraid to acknowledge it. Once you do, it makes you vulnerable to pain. And I know you suffered a great deal when your mother left you. But she came back. That's what love is. Highs and lows. Joy and sorrow. But it's worth every risk."

Heat suffused her cheeks at the audacity of her words.

She waited for equally heated words to rain down on her head, but none came. He kept staring at the sprig.

"At nineteen I knew what I wanted," Cait told him, "but I couldn't force you to love me, so I ended the engagement. That wasn't easy to do. My father practically disowned me, but I still couldn't give in." She swallowed and said the words she needed to say. "I'm sorry if I hurt you."

He lifted his head and a rare glimpse of a smile lit his face. "I think hell just froze over."

Her mouth twitched in response. "I do remember saying hell would freeze over before I'd ever apologize. But I'm tired of this fighting. You want revenge? Go ahead. Give it everything you've got. But you are not blameless."

"Maybe not," he muttered, and leaned back in the grass. He crossed his booted feet as if he and Cait were having a pleasant relaxing afternoon instead of reliving the engagement from hell. His snakeskin boots were dark brown and bespoke high-dollar comfort. She glanced down at her scuffed, worn ones caked with cow crap. What a difference.

Her eyes were drawn to his long legs and manhood, outlined by the tight Wranglers. It made her acutely aware of the difference between the sexes.

He gazed at her. "The night you visited Whiskey Red you said something about a magical shoe. What did you mean?"

It was hard to look away from the warmth she saw in his eyes, so she didn't. "That was silly."

"I want to know."

She swallowed. "When I ran from the party, I

lost a high heel. You know the Cinderella story. Maddie brought me the shoe and, being the romantic she is, said that all I had to do was slip it on and you would love me. Fairy-tale stuff."

"Did you believe?"

Like a fool.

"No. I've outgrown that." She bluffed like a Vegas poker player. A palpable silence stretched, as taut as her nerves. "May I ask you a question?"

"I suppose."

"Why did you ever agree to marry me?"

He sat up and rested a forearm on a knee. "Have you looked in the mirror?"

Astonishment hit her in the face like a handful of manure. "You agreed to the marriage because I'm easy on the eyes."

"Mostly. And the marriage would have been beneficial to Southern Cross and High Five."

"Oh, yeah, that really makes my heart flutter."

"I don't get it. You're fighting tooth and nail to save High Five now, but back then you walked away from it."

"High Five wasn't in trouble then."

"It wouldn't be now if you had stayed."

"But would we still be together?" She fired back the question, her voice as fervent as a preacher's on Sunday morning. "Without love, how would our marriage have survived?"

He lifted his shoulders. "Does any marriage come with a guarantee?"

"No, but love always beats the odds."

"Sometimes. Sometimes it muddles the situation."

"Not in my opinion. It makes it stronger."

"Whatever." He waved a hand. "It makes no difference now. Your father has pitted us against each other and I will honor the agreement I made with him."

Judd rose to his feet and blew out a hard breath. "We can't go back and change the past, and we certainly can't start over. We've hurt each other too much."

"Uh-huh." She waited for an apology from him, something to ease the ache in her heart. She waited in vain.

He held out a hand and she placed hers in his big palm. He pulled her to her feet. "I'm tired of the fighting, too." He gazed off into the distance with a thoughtful expression. "Yes, I admit I wanted revenge in the worst way, and I intended to make you pay for walking away from me and everything I'd offered you. What woman would do that? I knew without a doubt you'd come back begging." His big chest expanded with a sigh. "You never did."

"Did you want me to?" she asked, and held her breath.

His expression changed. "I'm not sure *want* is the right word. I never thought about you or your feelings. My father said you'd come crawling back and I believed him. A woman has to know her place in life."

"Do you still believe that rubbish?"

He heaved another sigh. "No. The years and Caitlyn Belle have slowly altered my mind-set. I can't say I've changed completely. Like you said, those ideas were drilled into me. I'm making progress with my mother. I give in to her because I don't want to hurt her feelings. That has to be progress."

"Yes. I believe it is. It means you care about her, and caring leads to love."

"Ah, yeah, that infamous four-letter word. Keep your dreams, Caitlyn. You deserve them. For me, that elusive emotion is just that—elusive."

"It doesn't have to be."

"Oh, yes, it does. My scars are too deep." His jaw tightened. "But I don't have to live with this anger and resentment anymore. I don't hate you, but like I said, your father has put me in the middle of High Five's affairs, and in six months we'll assess the situation and take it from there."

"You don't think I can make this ranch show a profit, do you?"

"The odds are against you. It's been in debt too long."

She bit her lip to keep words locked in her throat.

"Take the money, Caitlyn, and find the man you want. He's not here."

She wanted to smack him, shake him and, to her surprise, hug him. In a moment of clarity she realized the man she wanted was standing in front of her. And as before, he didn't love her. With her heart somewhere in her crappy boots she walked toward Jaz.

"Caitlyn." She turned back. "Your father would have been proud of you today."

Ironically, those weren't the words she wanted to hear. Her heart had been hoping for so much more. The fairy tale loomed just out of her reach.

She swung into the saddle and headed for home. Love was something he wasn't willing to give or didn't know how to give. The years stretched ahead, lonely and empty. High Five had to survive. That's what she was fighting for. But it wasn't enough.

She still wanted it all.

JUDD WATCHED HER ride away and marveled at what a sincere apology had triggered in him. He'd mellowed. Some would say like a lovesick pup, but he knew that wasn't the case. The honest fact was he didn't enjoy hurting her.

Maybe there was hope for him.

He wasn't good at sharing, and today he'd shared more with her than he ever had with anyone. It was a start, and maybe someday he'd understand what that love she talked about meant.

He seriously doubted it, though. That emotion hadn't been ingrained in him from birth. And he didn't know if it was something a man could learn.

For the first time in his life, he wanted to.

He reached for Baron's reins and headed for Southern Cross. Harland and the cowboys would be quitting for the day. Caitlyn and the bull would be the topic of conversation. He had a feeling she'd been elevated a few notches in their eyes.

It would certainly cut back on Harland's antagonism of her. Judd was sure the man was responsible for a lot of incidents that happened on High Five, like the broken fences and the broken windmill. He couldn't prove it, but the moment he could, Harland would be gone from Southern Cross. He'd worked many years for Judd's dad, and out of respect for those years Judd gave the man the benefit of the doubt.

He dismounted and handed a cowboy his reins. "Take care of Baron."

"Yes, sir." The cowhand led the horse away.

"I didn't have to shoot that bull, after all," Harland said, his tone boastful. "I never thought Miss Belle had it in her."

"You've underestimated Caitlyn Belle."

The gloating left his face. "Your father wouldn't think so. He wouldn't like a woman running High Five."

"My father doesn't run this ranch anymore."

"I know. But he wouldn't kowtow to no woman."

Judd's body became rigid as he tried to control his anger. "I'm telling you for the last time to leave Miss Belle alone. Southern Cross is your business, not High Five. Do I make myself clear?"

"Yes, sir."

"Then get the stables cleaned out and I'll attend to Whiskey Red."

"I can give the horse a workout," Chuck, an eager young cowboy, volunteered.

"No one touches that horse."

"Yes, sir." The young man stepped back.

Judd didn't have to apologize for his actions. He owned this place, but suddenly his blasted conscience was kicking in again, like a buzzing mosquito he wanted to swat. He wasn't sure why it was being exercised more than usual.

His father had never apologized in his life, and never cared one iota what the cowhands thought of him. He'd hired and fired them at will. It was a plan that worked well.

Until now.

There was something about respect that had to be earned. His father had never cared about respect. He had bought that, too. But Judd wanted to be different. And he started now.

Or maybe he had started earlier, with Caitlyn.

"Chuck," he called as the cowboy strolled away, his head bowed. "Feed Whiskey, lead her into the corral and let her walk around. I'll be out later."

"Yes, sir." The boy seemed to bounce in his boots as he hurried to the stables.

"You can't be easy on these hands." Harland spit chewing tobacco into the dirt. "They'll take advantage."

"That's my business."

The foreman saluted and walked into the barn.

Judd made his way to the house. He should check in at the office, but Brenda Sue would be there and he wasn't in the mood. Ron, his office manager, was hard of hearing and tuned Brenda Sue out without much of a problem.

In his study, Judd grabbed the bourbon and a shot glass. Before he could pour it, the door swung open and Brenda Sue breezed in.

Damn, the woman was like lint—hard to get rid of and aggravating in the process.

"Oh, Judd, glad you're back. Ron wants you to look at these grain prices. The supplier raised 'em because gasoline and diesel are so high, and he thinks they're sticking it to you. I know what he means about that. My ex-husband sticks it to me every chance he gets. He's supposed to have the kids two weeks this summer, but now he says he can only do one week. Bullshit, I told him. They're his kids and he needs to spend time with them. I need a break. And my parents are griping that *they* need a break. I feel like a damn pincushion and—"

"Shut up!"

She drew back. "Oh, you're in one of those moods."

He glared at her and yanked the papers from her hand. "I'll get together with Ron on this."

"I don't know why you have to be so rude."

Did the woman not have a clue?

"You sound like my ex," she continued. "He was always yelling at me to shut up."

Judd bet the man had a constant headache. His skull was ringing in just five minutes.

"I don't know why people are so mean to me."

He sat down, and there went his conscience again, knocking on his door. Damn woman. He didn't care about her problems. He didn't want to hear one more word about her or her life. He just wanted her to do her job. Could she really not know how annoying she was?

He picked up a pen and twirled it between his fingers. "I'm going to tell you something and I want you to listen. Don't speak. Do you understand?"

"I'm not an idiot."

"You talk all the time. You never even take a breath. Everything is about you and your life, and it gets annoying. If you don't want people to be rude to you, stop talking so much, and listen."

"I don't do that, but my ex said something similar. He was always rude, though. That was his personality. I talk a lot, I know, but that's me. I just talk and—"

He held up a hand. "Stop."

She stomped a foot. "I can't." Her face fell. "Oh, no. It's true."

"Judd, are you here?" His mother's voice echoed from the hallway.

"Just ask a question and wait for a response. That's all you have to do. Count to ten or something."

Brenda Sue smiled, and that was the last thing Judd wanted to see. He didn't want her getting any ideas about a personal relationship between them.

"You can be quite nice sometimes."

"Just do your job and try not to annoy me with incessant chatter."

"Judd…" His mother paused in the doorway, her eyes going from him to Brenda Sue. "Is there a reason you always seem to be in Judd's study?"

"Yes, ma'am. I work for him." She said the words slowly, as if talking to a child, and then walked out without saying another word.

Hot damn. Maybe Brenda Sue did have an off switch.

Renee's eyes narrowed. "You're not getting involved with her, are you?"

"No, Mom, I can honestly say without a shadow of a doubt that I am not."

"Good." She took a seat in a leather chair and crossed her legs. "You haven't said two words to me since the ball."

"And you wouldn't want to hear those two words." He poured the bourbon. "How about a drink?"

"No, thank you." Renee looked at him. "You can act as mad as you want, but I know you enjoyed the party, especially your dance with Caitlyn."

He downed the shot. "I'm not in a mood to talk about that horrid ball."

"What do you want to talk about?"

"Nothing."

"Surprise, surprise."

"Don't be cute." He fingered the glass. Since his talk with Caitlyn, a lot of thoughts had been running through his mind. And a lot of them were about his parents. Their relationship. He couldn't believe the question that mingled with the bourbon on his tongue.

"You told me a number of times how you and Dad got back together."

"Yes."

God, he needed more liquor to ask this question. He poured another shot and downed it. "Did Dad ever tell you that…that he loved you?"

Her eyes opened wide. Clearly, she was shocked. He was feeling a bit of that himself.

She scooted her chair closer, as if she was going to reveal some deep dark secret. "No. Not in all the years I was married to him did he ever say those words."

"Did it bother you?"

"Damn right, it did. It was the main reason I left the first time. That and his affairs. A woman can only take so much."

"Other than the fact that you would get to see me again, what did he say to make you marry him the second time around?"

"Well." She tapped a pink fingernail against her cheek. "I was working in a diner in Abilene at the time. He just walked in and I almost lost the cookies I'd had for a snack that afternoon. He sat in my section so I had to wait on him. It wasn't like, 'Oh, golly gee, this is my lucky day.' It was more like, 'You rotten, sorry bastard.'"

"So you had words?"

"Hell, no. I wanted to see my son, so I plastered a smile on my face and asked what he wanted in my sweetest, softest voice."

"And?"

"He looked me up and down and said I was still the best goddamn looking woman he'd ever seen. Then he glanced out the window at the motel across the street and said how about a quickie for old times' sake."

"Did you slap his face?"

"Son, I don't think you're getting the picture. It had been seven years since I'd seen you, and he could have demeaned me any way he wanted as long as he let me see my son."

"So you had sex with him?"

"Not before we worked out a deal. I knew he'd divorced Blanche, and I was ready to come home. We spent that evening and the night together. The next morning he asked if I wanted to get married. He made it very plain that was the only way I could see you. We flew to Vegas, did the deed and returned to Southern Cross."

It sounded so cold, so unemotional. Just like Judd was. Just like his father had been.

Judd glanced out the window to the miles and miles of Southern Cross. His heritage, his birthright.

He brought his gaze back to his mother. "Did you love him?"

"At times. At others I hated him, but we were good together. We understood each other and he didn't cheat again. I nursed him in his last days when he was dying of pancreatic cancer. I thought it was love until I saw the will."

His father had left her an allowance, and permission to live at Southern Cross until her death. If she remarried, she received nothing.

"If I had known what he had in mind, I would have wrapped that oxygen tubing around his neck and choked the life out of him before the good Lord could take his sorry soul."

Judd could see so clearly that his and Caitlyn's marriage would have been the same. He would have browbeaten her at every turn until she'd bowed to his every wish. *Oh, God.* A chill shuddered through him. He didn't know much about love, but he knew it wasn't like that.

He swallowed hard and met his mother's eyes and said what he had to, what he should have said years ago. "I'm sorry I was mean to you when you came home."

"Oh, Judd, my son." She jumped up and ran

around the desk and hugged him. For the first time, he hugged her back.

"Don't be like him. Please don't be like him."

He made a vow to himself that he wouldn't. But he knew it wouldn't be easy.

CHAPTER SIXTEEN

"HOW COULD SOMETHING like that happen?"

They sat in Cait's office going over the day's events. Maddie was appalled at Boss's injury, and Cait tried to explain it as best as she could. "It was just a freak accident."

"Couldn't you have called a vet? Why did you have to shoot him?"

Guilt scraped across her conscience and her stomach clenched. She knew Maddie didn't mean it that way. Her city-raised sister was not accustomed to the hard knocks and plain bad luck of ranch life. How could Cait make her understand?

"There was nothing a vet could have done. The bull was in excruciating pain. His penis had been split open by the barbed wire. I worked at a vet clinic in college and I know even a prize bull would have been put down."

"How did you do it?" Maddie shivered in her chair.

"I was shaking so badly I didn't know if I could

hold the rifle steady, but somehow I managed. No way was I going to back down in front of Harland and his boys. But most of all I could see how much pain Boss was in, and it was up to me to end his misery."

"I could never have done it."

"It's amazing what you can do in a crisis." Cait reached down and pulled off a boot. Her feet were beginning to hurt, along with her backside and every other part of her. She placed both boots to the side. "I'm dog tired, and I need a bath to wash away the trauma of this day. And maybe a bottle of wine."

"Remember the last time you drank a lot of wine," Maddie stated with an impish grin.

"Yeah." She closed her eyes briefly as she recalled the heady feeling of kissing Judd. Today she'd wanted to do the same thing. He was understanding, compassionate—just like the man she knew he was under all that male-superiority rhetoric.

"What did y'all do with Boss?"

"When Coop got back from hauling the calves to auction, we took a tractor and buried him beneath a cottonwood on Crooked Creek. We don't usually bury an animal, but Boss's body was probably riddled with infection, and I thought it best. He can see his herd from a very shady spot."

"Ranching is hard work," Maddie remarked.

"Yeah." Cait looked at her sister. "And I'm going to need your help."

"Anything, just so it's not gruesome. I do not do the gun thing."

On the outside, Maddie acted soft and fragile, but she was a Belle and would do what she had to—just as Cait had.

"This doesn't require a gun. Tomorrow Gil Bardwell's crew will start loading sand and gravel from our property. I'll be elsewhere on the ranch and I was hoping you could keep an eye on them."

"Okay."

"We're being paid by the weight. Mr. Bardwell has a scale at his plant, and they weigh the truck empty, and then again after it's loaded. He seems like a nice enough fellow, but somehow expecting him to be one hundred percent honest about what he hauls out seems a little too trusting. If you could take my truck and check on the operation, keep track of the number of loads you see going out, that would help. He would know we're watching and he wouldn't be tempted to cheat us."

"Now that I can handle."

"No bloodshed at all." Cait removed the rubber band from her hair and wiggled her fingers through the French braid, loosening it. "Gran seemed fine at supper."

"I think she's much better."

"She's happy you're here, and maybe we won't see any more of these dressing up…" Her voice trailed away as their grandmother appeared in the doorway, leaning on the jamb.

"'Come up and see me sometime.'" She wore a frilly short skirt and equally revealing top, with fishnet stockings and heels. Her long white hair tumbled down her back.

Oh, crap! Cait didn't need this tonight.

"Mae West, remember?" Dorie asked gleefully.

"Let's go upstairs, Gran." Maddie took her arm.

"What's wrong with you girls? You used to love playing dress-up."

Cait stood with a tired sigh. "We've outgrown it, Gran." And there was the little matter of the big bad wolf at their door, which made play-acting seem immature.

"Now, that's just sad. You're never too old to remember being young."

Cait took her other arm. "Okay, Gran." But Cait felt she might have to dig deep and use dynamite to retrieve that feeling. Tonight she felt tired and completely used up.

As they made their way upstairs, she wondered if this would be the scenario for the rest of her life. Would she be old before her time and never remember the carefree days of her youth?

Suddenly those feelings she'd had as she'd

worn the red dress fluttered over her—she was feminine, young and desirable. She'd experienced an exhilaration that was hard to forget.

Especially when she'd seen the look in Judd's eyes.

Maybe she was just tired, but tonight she would store that memory as a keepsake close to her heart.

Heaven only knew when she'd feel that way again.

JULY SNEAKED IN on sultry waves of suffocating heat, and Texas felt like the bowels of hell. Every day God seemed to stoke that fire a little more as the ground dried and cracked and the grasses turned a dusty brown.

But cattle and horses had to have water and feed, so ranchers had to work. Each day seemed to grow longer and hotter as they settled into a routine. Maddie took care of Gran and the selling of the sand and gravel. She was very organized, keeping notes and numbers in a small notebook. Mr. Bardwell wasn't going to slip a load by her.

Cooper had fixed the transmission on Cait's truck, so she didn't have to worry about Maddie careening off into a ditch somewhere.

Maddie was also getting a tan, and had gained weight from Etta's cooking. She looked healthy again, Cait was glad to see.

Cait worked her butt off most days and didn't have time to think about anything beyond keeping High Five afloat. She'd received a good price for the calves, but if the county didn't get rain soon, calf prices would drop.

She was actually able to pay Cooper, Rufus and Etta a decent salary this month. That was a satisfying feeling. She had to keep working, though.

Since the bull incident, she hadn't seen Judd. As he'd said, her father had now pitted them against each other. Even in death, Dane Belle was controlling her life. And she had to wonder how long she would continue to try to prove him wrong.

As A BOY, Judd had worked on the ranch as a cowboy, but then he went to college and came home with a degree. His father put him to work managing the business, and he missed cowboying. Jack Calhoun had planned his only son's future, and Judd never wavered from that vision.

Southern Cross was a big responsibility, yet he took it on because it was expected of him. But after talking to Caitlyn and his mother, he found life taking a detour. He now firmly believed Renee had a right to a share of Southern Cross. She had earned it in more ways than he had ever imagined. He also knew that Caitlyn had had good reason to end their engagement.

Admitting that had taken a hefty amount of bourbon, sleepless nights and more soul searching than he was used to. Revenge faded into the background, and his goal now was to be able to live with himself, his choices and his decisions.

After much thought, he offered his mother half of the ranch. With tears in her eyes, she declined. That he'd suggested it was all she needed, she told him, and to know her son thought that much of her—as his mother and as a woman.

Making things right with Caitlyn wasn't so easy. Judd couldn't just gift her the royalties. The big expense of buying the rights was already putting a strain on Southern Cross finances. His conscience, his ever-growing nemesis, knocked on his heart daily with a reminder that he needed to talk to Caitlyn. But he kept putting it off.

He threw himself into working on the ranch, much to Harland's chagrin. The foreman told him repeatedly he could handle things, and Judd had to wonder why his presence made the man so antsy.

One day, watching from a hill, he saw Caitlyn ride across the High Five. There was no mistaking her curved body. She was putting everything she had into making that ranch survive. No man could do a better job.

He also saw the dump trucks going in and out

daily. She'd found a way to make money, and he admired her determination and ingenuity. He admired *her*.

Soon he had to tell her that.

THERE WAS A HURRICANE gathering force on the Gulf Coast and rain was expected for the area. It was the best news Cait had heard in a while—not the winds, but the rain.

She dismounted at a stock pond and realized that within a month the pond would be dry. They'd have to move the cows to another pasture or pipe water from a nearby well. Or sell. Her stomach tightened at that prospect.

She'd make that decision later in the week. She swung back into the saddle and took a moment to wipe the sweat from her brow. Damn, it was hot! But it was late afternoon, and the force of the heat was ebbing as the giant fireball sank slowly toward the western horizon. She could almost hear a sigh from the landscape.

Suddenly, she heard riders coming. She was close to the Southern Cross fence line, so it had to be cowboys from there. With an uneasy feeling in her gut, she turned Jaz toward the sound.

She guided the horse out of the clearing into the woods, heading toward the fence. The fact that this might not be a good idea crossed her mind.

She was a woman alone, and Harland and his cowboys weren't all that friendly. Just like shooting Boss, though, she had to be able to handle every situation that arose.

Beyond the thicket she could see horses and riders. She pulled up and looked closer. They were gazing at something near the fence. And they were too close for her comfort.

What were they doing?

She pulled the rifle from the saddle scabbard, clicked off the safety and rode forward. Stopping about forty feet away, she took in the situation. A dead Southern Cross Brahman lay right at the fence. A newborn calf had somehow maneuvered beneath the barbed wire and was now on High Five land. It lay prone. She wasn't sure if it was dead or alive. Cait rode closer.

Harland and a cowboy she'd never seen before had dismounted and were inspecting the cow.

"Miss Belle." Harland tipped his hat and looked beyond her. "Your boy Yates not with you?"

"What's going on here?" His nasty remark made her edgy, but she kept it out of her voice.

"This is none of your concern, Miss Belle." He dragged out her name like a prisoner would a ball and chain—slow and hard.

She pointed with the barrel of the rifle. "That calf is on my property."

"Why don't you go paint your nails or something and leave this to me."

The cowboy laughed.

Anger zigzagged through her. Her hand tightened on the rifle and she kept her eyes squarely on Harland. "I'm asking you one more time… what happened here?"

Harland glanced at the cowboy on his right, and she wasn't sure what was going to happen next. She was just grateful the fence was between them.

"One of our pregnant heifers got out of the corral, and this is where we found her—dead. From the signs of struggle on the ground it must have been a difficult birth, and the calf slid under the fence."

Cait's eyes were drawn to the trembling baby. It was alive. She also noticed something else—the calf was black, not white like the Brahman.

As if Harland read her mind, he said, "Must be an offspring from that damn black bull of yours."

"Must be," she murmured.

"Mr. Calhoun is not going to be pleased about this. The heifer is dead and that calf is worthless. We'll knock it in the head and be on our way." Harland nodded to the cowboy.

What? The mere thought of such a senseless, cruel act ricocheted through her, triggering more anger and a double dose of determination. No one was killing the calf.

The cowhand moved forward, grabbed a fence post and was about to swing himself over when Cait pointed the rifle at him. "Cross that fence and you're a dead man."

The cowboy's boots hit the ground with a thud.

"C'mon, Miss Belle, you're not gonna shoot nobody." Harland glared at her.

"And nobody's killing this calf."

"It belongs to Southern Cross."

"It's on High Five and was sired by my bull."

Harland moved toward the fence with an evil glint in his shady eyes. "Listen, little lady, you're interfering in something that don't concern you, and if you value your life, you'll turn that horse around and get the hell out of here."

Fear mingled with her anger, but no way would she turn tail and run.

She nudged Jaz closer, her eyes on Harland, the gun pointed at his chest. "Want to try your luck, Harland? Go ahead and try to cross the fence."

His face turned beet red. "You bitch." He glanced at the cowboy standing next to him. "Kill that calf, and I don't care what you do to her."

A wicked grin spread across the cowboy's face as he again reached for the cedar post.

Cait leveled the gun on him. "I'm not too particular where I place this bullet. And if you think I won't shoot, just keep on coming."

Once again the cowboy slid back to the ground, his hand unconsciously going to his crotch. "I'm not getting shot for a no-good calf."

"You bastard!" Harland shouted at him. "Saddle up, we're getting out of here." He grabbed his horse's reins and swung up, his eyes on Caitlyn. "You haven't heard the last of this. Judd Calhoun will want answers."

"He knows where I live."

She relaxed her grip on the rifle as she watched the riders disappear in a cloud of dust. In case they had a plan of circling back, she kept watching. Satisfied, she dismounted to take a closer look.

She squatted and laid the rifle in the leaves as she looked over the animal. It was a bull calf, still covered in mucus from the birth. His coat was matted with it. The mother hadn't had a chance to lick him dry.

The calf made a croaking sound deep in his throat. Cait grabbed a handful of leaves and started to rub his body to clean it. The newborn shivered, but she continued, trying to evoke a fighting spirit in the animal.

"C'mon, little one, lift your head, root around for milk. Aren't you hungry? C'mon."

He didn't move.

She had to get him back to the barn. But how?

Cooper and Rufus were on the other side of the ranch, and if she left to go get them, she feared Harland and his boys would come back.

A buzzard landed on the fence. Then another.

Damn! She threw a stick at them. "Shoo," she yelled. They flew away, but she knew the vultures would be back, with more of their friends.

She stood and surveyed the situation. If she was a man, she could just lift the calf onto Jaz and ride for home. But she didn't have that much upper body strength. Her mind was as sharp as any man's, though, and she could figure this out.

Jaz was the solution.

She whistled and the horse trotted forward. "Okay, girl." She stroked her face. "I need your help." She pulled on the reins to bring her to her knees.

It didn't work. Jaz threw up her head and backed away.

Damn it! Whiskey Red would have knelt in a heartbeat. But Red didn't belong to her anymore.

She took the reins again. "Jaz, I can only get the calf on your back if you kneel down. C'mon, girl, you can do it." With her booted toe, Cait tapped the back of Jaz's knee. "Down, girl, down."

She kept resisting. Cait kept pushing.

Finally, to her surprise, Jaz's front knees buckled and she went to the ground. "Good girl, good girl. Stay. Don't move. Don't move." She had to hurry. Jaz wouldn't stay in that position long.

Wrapping both arms around the calf's body, she tried to stand up, and fell back on her butt. Damn. The newborn weighed more than she had expected. *Okay.* She got back to her feet, determined to save this calf. It would be her redemption for having to shoot Boss.

This time she counted to three, then lifted with her knees and half dragged, half carried the calf to Jaz. Once again she took a deep breath and hoisted with all her strength. The front legs slid across Jaz's withers and Cait pushed until the calf was draped in front of the saddle. She could get him to the barn like this.

Slowly holding the calf secure, she prompted Jaz to rise. Then she slid her rifle into the scabbard and quickly swung into the saddle, gripping him with one hand.

"Let's go home," she said, and they trotted out of the woods, across pastures and through a hay field. Sweat trickled down her face, but she didn't have a free hand to wipe it away. Soon she saw the ranch buildings, and hoped it wasn't too late to save the animal's life.

JUDD DROVE THROUGH High Cotton on his way home. Walker was at the gas station and he waved for him to stop. Judd pulled in.

The constable strolled to the driver's side. "Have you been home?" he asked.

"No. I'm headed there now. Why?"

"I just got a call from Harland. There's been an incident and he wanted to let me know."

"What happened?"

"One of your heifers that was about to calf got out of the corral, and they found her near High Five. The cow was dead and Caitlyn took the calf."

"What? Why would Caitlyn take it, and why in the hell was the heifer out of her pen? We watch them round the clock when they're about to calf. They're too damn expensive to lose. Something's not right."

"I was on my way over there to investigate when I saw your truck."

"Good. I'll meet you there." Judd turned toward the High Five.

Why would Caitlyn take a Southern Cross calf? That didn't make any sense. She wasn't a cattle rustler. He'd been putting off talking to her and now he had no choice.

He just wished it wasn't under these circumstances.

CHAPTER SEVENTEEN

CAIT RODE INTO THE BARN and Maddie followed her. Maddie had taken to checking on Bardwell's crew on horseback. She was beginning to enjoy riding and the everyday work on the ranch.

Cait dismounted and her sister was right there, staring at the newborn animal. "What in the world? Where did that come from? Is it dead? What are—"

"Stop with the twenty questions and help me unload him."

They both grabbed hold and stumbled backward into the hay. But the calf was safely on the ground.

"Where's Cooper?" Cait asked, checking the newborn. He lay still, unmoving, but he was breathing. She had to keep him that way.

"I guess they haven't come in yet," Maddie replied.

"Keep an eye on this little one. I have to fix some milk." Cait headed for the supply room, where the sink and refrigerator were located.

"What do you want me to do?" Maddie shouted after her.

"Get a rag and rub him. Talk to him."

Cait found the powered milk and a bottle. After mixing the powder with water, she poured it into the bottle and attached the nipple. Hurrying back, she knelt in the hay.

"I've rubbed and rubbed, but he's not moving or responding," Maddie told her, a note of anxiety in her voice. "I think he's almost dead."

"We have to give him a little incentive." She lifted his head into her lap and attempted to pry his jaws apart.

Judd and Walker entered the barn, but Cait didn't look up. She kept trying to get the calf to open his mouth.

"Caitlyn," Walker said.

"Yeah. What is it?"

"Harland said you took a Southern Cross calf."

She glanced up then, her eyes stormy. "Does this look like a Southern Cross calf?"

"Nope, certainly doesn't."

Judd saw the expression on her face—one of love and determination. Caitlyn always fought for what she loved, except when it came to him.

"Here." She handed Maddie the bottle. "When I open his mouth, put the nipple in."

"Okay." Her sister grasped the bottle, but as

hard as they tried, the calf would not take the nipple.

Judd stepped around Walker and knelt by Maddie. "They can be stubborn." He took the bottle and glanced into Caitlyn's glaring blue eyes. "May I?"

"I suppose."

"Sometimes they just need to taste the milk or smell it." He squirted milk around the calf's nose. "Open his mouth," he instructed Cait. When it parted a fraction, he slipped the nipple in and squirted some more.

The little animal's head moved and a grunting sound left his throat.

"He's moving," Maddie cried with excitement.

Judd placed his hand over Caitlyn's and together they worked the calf's jaws around the nipple. His throat moved. He swallowed. They kept working until the calf twitched his head, as if to butt an udder, and sucked on his own.

Maddie leaped to her feet. "Oh, this is so exciting. He's going to live."

Once the calf started sucking, he struggled to get to his feet. Cait scrambled away, holding on to the animal with one hand, as did Judd. The baby was unstable, but finally managed to stand. After a couple of minutes he sank back into the hay, but held up his head, looking around.

Maddie made herself comfortable beside him, stroking him and cooing.

Judd saw Walker eyeing her strangely. Without moving his gaze from Maddie, Walker asked Caitlyn, "Is this the calf Harland was talking about?"

"Yes."

"But—"

"What's going on?" Judd asked before Walker could.

Caitlyn relayed a story that had his eyebrow twitching upward. "Harland was going to kill the calf?"

She nodded. "That's what he said."

"How did you stop him?" Walker asked.

Cait's chin lifted. "With my rifle."

The lawman winced.

"I have a right to protect my property, and this calf is half mine. My bull sired it."

"He's also half mine," Judd stated.

Her eyes flared. "You're not taking this calf so Harland can kill it."

"I didn't say that."

"Then what are you saying?"

"That I need to find out what's going on. Where did you find the heifer and the calf?"

"Near the old Dry Gulch Road."

"I thought that road was closed."

"It's supposed to be, but people still use it."

"I'll check it out in the morning. It's too dark now."

Cait rested back on her heels. "What do you want to do about the calf?"

"You're giving me a choice?"

"Maybe." Her eyes twinkled. "If it's the right choice."

"Figured that." He stood. "Keep the calf for now and we'll talk about it later." His eyes caught hers. "Would you mind keeping this under your hat?"

She reached for her hat in the hay and slapped it against her thigh. "Nothing much in here, anyway. It could use a little company." Her smile made him dizzy, weak and feeling luckier than he had in a very long time.

"Thanks." He strolled toward his truck with a long-forgotten smile.

JUDD PARKED BEHIND WALKER at the Southern Cross. Getting out of his truck, he said, "Let's go inside. We need to talk."

Walker followed him into the study, where Judd grabbed the bourbon and two glasses. "How about a drink?"

"No, thanks," he replied. "With two kids, I've had to cut back."

Judd placed the bottle on the desk and eased into his chair. "I know what you mean. I've been drinking a hell of a lot lately."

"When Trisha left me and the kids, I thought liquor could solve all my troubles. But I soon found out that wasn't the answer. My kids needed me, even though at times my daughter seems to hate me."

"How's the situation now?"

"After living in Houston, my daughter despises Hicksville, as she calls it. My son just wants his mama."

Judd knew that feeling and had an urge to reach for the bottle. He didn't. "That's rough," he replied, eyeing the amber liquid. "Have you divorced Trisha?"

"Yep." Walker folded his hands between his knees. "When your wife runs off with another man, it's a safe bet the marriage is over. I mailed the divorce papers to her sister in Lubbock, like Trisha requested. It's officially over. But it's hell trying to explain that to my kids."

"I'm glad you came home to High Cotton."

"Me, too." Walker smiled slightly. "It's good being back with old friends." The smile widened. "In high school we were something. Judd and Walker—the studs."

"That was just hype."

"Yeah." Walker rubbed his hands. "But as teen-agers without a clue, we ate it up."

Old memories mingled with the quiet in the room.

"So what do you want me to do about the calf?" Walker asked, and held up a hand. "And just so we're clear—I'm not taking that calf away from Caitlyn. You'll have to do that one yourself."

"Afraid she'll pull a gun on you?"

"Hell, no. It's that sister of hers and the evil eye she keeps giving me. She's treating that calf like a baby, and she looks at me as the enemy."

Judd laughed. "Maddie's an angel."

"Yeah, right."

Judd leaned forward. "Forget about the calf. I'm more concerned how that heifer got out of the pen and so far away without anyone noticing."

"You think something fishy is going on?"

"You bet I do. See what you can find out about Brahman heifers being sold at any auction barns across the state, even private buyers. Every one of my heifers has a Southern Cross brand, so it shouldn't take long to find out if they've been sold without my permission."

"I'll get on it first thing in the morning." Walker stood. "I might even make some calls tonight."

"Thanks. I appreciate it."

"Any idea who'd have enough nerve to do such a thing?"

"Harland." Judd pushed himself to his feet and stretched his shoulders. "He's resented me since my father's death. He thought I would give him free rein with the ranch, as my dad had. I told him things were going to be different and I wanted to be consulted on everything. He wasn't happy, and I think he's trying to show me I don't run this ranch. I will now be checking the books and every aspect of this operation."

"Watch your back."

"Will do."

Judd sank into his chair, staring at the bourbon bottle. But what he saw were blue forget-me-not eyes. And they were smiling.

THE HOUSE WAS QUIET as Cait sneaked down the stairs. She tiptoed to the kitchen and slipped out the back door.

At the barn, she sat in the hay, watching the baby calf, which Cooper had put in one of the horse stalls. The animal was sleeping, his head curved to the side. He was going to make it. Some good had come out of this day.

She'd been so scared facing Harland. She still wasn't sure what she would have done if the cowboy had crossed the fence. Shooting a person, even if he was as mean as a rattlesnake, was a whole different deal—and came with a whole different realm of emotions.

It ain't women's work.

A hiccup of laughter left her throat. *Nope.* Glancing up, she saw the red high heel on the shelf, highlighted by the single lightbulb hanging from the rafters. She closed her eyes and envisioned herself in Judd's arms, dancing close together.

She swayed slightly to the music in her head, remembering the touch of his hands, his lips.

"Caitlyn."

She opened her eyes and Judd stood there. She blinked and glanced around. Was she dreaming?

"I saw the light and figured you were here checking on the calf."

"Yeah." Scooting up against the wall, she brushed back her long hair. She should have known he wouldn't just forget about the situation.

"How's he doing?"

"I think he's going to live."

Judd removed his Stetson and eased down by her. She wished he hadn't. A tantalizing woodsy scent pulled at her senses. At her heart.

"What are we going to do about the calf?" he asked, placing his hat in the hay and resting his forearms on his knees.

"He was birthed on my property and sired by my bull, so I believe that makes him legally mine."

"The birthing part is up for question. No one saw that, and his mother belongs to Southern Cross. Custody always goes to the mother."

"The cow is dead," she pointed out.

"So what do we do? King Solomon would suggest cutting the calf in half. At that, you'd fold like a greenhorn in Vegas, so that pretty much gives me all the rights."

"Are you saying I'm weak?"

They glared at each other. The glares turned to smiles and then laughter. "Whoever takes the calf has a lot of work ahead, what with feeding and care."

"You're right," he said. "You can keep him."

"Thank you very much." She slapped Judd's shoulder playfully. "We could make a toast, but I forgot to bring wine this time."

"There's a better way to mark the agreement." Judd slipped his hand around her neck and drew her forward, his lips lightly touching, caressing, driving her crazy. She opened her mouth and the kiss deepened to a level they both needed.

"Caitie," he murmured, and her body turned to liquid, flowing only for him, as it had so many years ago when he'd called her that.

His fingers unsnapped her blouse and stroked her breast. Being deprived of him for so long, she felt as if she was drowning and he was the only one who could save her, with his touch, his hands.

"Judd," she whispered, and all her troubles, her worries, floated away.

He pressed her down in the hay and her hands feverishly sought his chest, his muscles. Without a second thought, she pulled his shirt from his jeans, needing more of him.

"Cait." He caught her hands and sank back against the wall. "We have to stop."

She felt deprived, lonely and a little angry. Pulling her shirt together, she sat up.

"We need to talk." He expelled a taut breath.

"Okay," she heard herself say, but her body was still craving something it wasn't going to get.

He ran both hands through his tousled hair. "You made the right choice in leaving me fourteen years ago."

If the ground had opened up and swallowed her she wouldn't have been any more surprised. He was apologizing—something she thought he would never, ever do.

"How do you know that?"

He picked up a blade of hay and studied it. "A lot of things. Getting to know you again and talking to my mom. My father drilled some hardcore beliefs into me at an early age, and I never saw life any differently."

She swallowed. "And you do now?"

He fiddled with the straw. "I'm getting there.

Slowly. I never thought I'd forgive my mother for leaving me when I was five." He drew a hard breath. "But I have. I'm finally able to listen and understand her side—why she did what she did."

"Judd, that's wonderful."

"All these years, the resentment kept building inside me, weighing me down, and when you left I thought you were just like my mother, and the weight became unbearable."

"Judd…"

He tucked her hair behind her ear, and at the gentle touch, her voice faded away.

"I couldn't understand why the women in my life wanted to get away from me. I naturally thought it was their fault, but sometimes in life you have to stop and look at the whole picture."

"And what did you see?"

His eyes met hers and she saw he was picturing the years, the good and the bad. A spiral of hope coiled around her heart.

"If you had married me, your life would have been just like my mother's. I would have controlled you, ruined your hopes and dreams, and within a year you would have bolted for freedom."

She trailed a finger down his nose. "You think so, huh?"

He reached up and locked his fingers with hers. "I know so. My father was wrong in his treatment of my mother. I was wrong in my treatment of you."

"I never thought I'd hear you say that."

His hand tightened on hers. "I never thought I'd say it, either. I wanted you to pay for having the gall to leave me."

"And now?" Her breath wedged in her throat.

He released her hand. *No. No. No.*

"As I said before, we can't go back and change things. Now we go on with our lives. I have no doubt at the end of six months High Five will be in the black. Dane was wrong. You can run this ranch."

Any other time, those words would have warmed the cockles of her heart. But not today. They weren't the words she wanted to hear.

"What if the ranch is in the red?"

"Then I'll honor the contract I made with your father."

"So nothing has changed?"

He dropped the straw with a sigh. "In that regard, no. Your father didn't want you to spend the rest of your life running this ranch, out every day in the saddle under a scorching sun or in the bitter cold. He wanted you to have a husband and kids. He wanted you to be pampered and have the best things in life."

She clenched her hands. "I've heard that before."

"Don't take this the wrong way, but what's so wrong with that?"

A hundred responses should have popped into her head, but only one made an appearance. "You think a woman's place is in the home and not as an equal partner."

"No. I think Caitlyn Belle can do anything she wants and stand toe to toe with any man. It's up to you to make up your mind what you really want."

Complete silence followed his words. Judd stretched his long legs out in front of him. The calf made a snoring sound and the night closed around them.

"You know what *I* want?" he asked.

"What?" She looked into his dark eyes and felt their magic.

"I'd like to lay you down in the hay and make love to you."

Her breath caught. "I want that, too."

His eyes held hers. "Are you sure?"

Say no. Just say no. Don't put your heart on the line again. Of its own volition, her hand reached up to touch his roughened cheek.

His eyes darkened to pitch-black. "Sweet Caitie, you're so tempting."

Her pulse accelerated at the passion in his gaze and in his voice.

"But it wouldn't solve anything, would it?"

Her pulse took a nosedive. She'd never expected him to be honorable.

"I guess not," she replied.

He swung to his feet before she realized his intent. "Hang on to your dreams, Caitlyn. You deserve a man who can love you completely."

She stared up at him. "What if you're that man?"

He expelled a breath. "I'm not. As I told you, I don't know a thing about the kind of love you need. The kind you deserve."

"We all know about love, Judd. It's something we're born with, but you have to be willing to open your heart to accept it. And to give it. It's really very simple."

"Not for me."

"As I told you before, love starts by caring. I bet you care about that black horse of yours."

"I sure do."

"You'd be hurt if something happened to him."

"I suppose."

"And your mom. You don't make waves because it would hurt her feelings. That's caring. That's loving. That's how it starts and grows. It's putting someone before yourself. It's trust and respect. It's a special connection between two people and it's felt in the heart—deeply. I know you've felt those emotions."

"Not the way you do, Caitie."

Words hung in her throat and she wanted to hit him, hug him, do anything to change his mind. Sadly, she realized he was the only who could change his way of thinking.

Judd glanced at the sleeping calf. "What are you going to name him?"

She thought for a second. "How about Solomon?"

"That works." He reached for his hat in the hay. Fitting it onto his head, he said, "Goodbye, Caitlyn." Then he turned and walked out of the barn.

She scrambled to her feet and watched as he strolled to his truck. Besides her family, High Five had always been the most important thing in her life. But now she wondered if it really was. A strange feeling settled on her. Had her father been right?

Was the man walking away more important to her than High Five?

Did she love Judd Calhoun that much?

CHAPTER EIGHTEEN

"CAIT."

Caitlyn jumped and pushed her palm to her chest. She'd been so engrossed in her thoughts she hadn't seen Maddie walk up. "You scared the crap out of me."

"Who's that leaving?" her sister asked, watching the taillights disappear down the road.

"Judd." Cait turned and went back into the barn.

"What did he want?"

She closed the gate of the stall. "He was checking on the calf."

"Is he going to let you keep him?"

"Yes." Cait flipped off the light and the barn was shrouded in darkness. "We named him Solomon."

"We did, huh?" Maddie remarked in a mocking tone as they strolled toward the house. "That's progress."

"Not really," Cait replied.

"Why not? No, don't answer. Wait."

They walked into the kitchen and Maddie hurried to the stove. "I'll make hot chocolate."

Cait frowned. "It's August in Texas."

She shrugged. "So? I just won't make it so hot."

"Whatever."

A few minutes later, Cait sat with a cup of hot chocolate in her hand, wondering if she should go raid the wine cabinet. She might need it to keep thoughts of Judd at bay.

The two sisters drank in silence.

"What did Judd say?" Maddie asked at last, eyeing Cait over the rim of her cup.

She took a long swallow. "He's not set on revenge anymore."

"Oh, Cait, that's wonderful."

"He's still buying High Five if it's not showing a profit, though."

"Oh."

"But he was different tonight."

"How?"

"He was genuinely sincere. He said Dad was wrong and I can run this ranch as good as any man."

"That was nice."

"Mmm." She placed her cup on the table. "But I didn't want him to be nice. I wanted him to throw me in the hay and make passionate love to me. I didn't want to think about profits, ranches or revenge. I just wanted to think about him and me. I wanted love to make a difference."

"But it doesn't to Judd?"

"No. He says he's incapable of the kind of love I want."

"Everyone's capable of love."

"Try telling that to Judd." She carried her cup to the sink. Leaning against the cabinet, she added, "The last couple of months I've been hoping that Judd and I could work out our differences. I never realized until tonight that I wanted the working out part to come with an I love you." She wrapped her arms around her waist. "I now know that's never going to happen. I'm going to be a lonely old spinster yearning for Judd Calhoun." She walked back to the table, gritting her teeth to keep from bursting into tears.

"Sometimes, and I say this from my vast experience—" Maddie rolled her eyes "—men don't know the difference between love and lust. I mean, you're never going to love anyone the way you love Judd, so wouldn't it be better to be with him than without him?"

"This from the eternal believer in love and fairy tales."

"Life sometimes changes our point of view."

"Mmm. But I can't see myself settling for anything less." Cait stood and linked her arm through Maddie's, pulling her to her feet. "Let's go to bed."

Arm in arm they walked toward the stairs. Halfway there Maddie stopped. "Oh, I came out to the barn to tell you that Sky called, but I got sidetracked."

"What did she have to say?"

"She said Todd's parents hired a P.I. and he was snooping around a diner not far from her apartment. So she and Kira are on the move again. She said she'd call when she found a safe place."

"Did you tell her to come home?"

"I did, and she said she'd think about it."

"Why can't she see this is the safest place?"

"Sky has to make her own decisions."

"Hopefully she'll turn up in the next day or two."

Later, Cait tossed and turned. Her thoughts were on Judd. Tonight was the final goodbye. He knew it and so did she. That's why he hadn't made love to her. He didn't want to complicate the issue.

Tomorrow her broken heart would start to mend—once again. Tomorrow she would continue her quest to save High Five. That was all she had now—a lot of empty tomorrows.

A choking sob left her throat and soon the tears followed. She made no move to stop them. They were what she needed at this moment in time.

JUDD SPENT A RESTLESS night, but was in his office early. All night he'd kept wondering if he'd lost his mind. Caitlyn wanted to make love and he'd said no. Why had he done that?

Make love?

He just caught his choice of words. It wasn't love. It was sex—nothing but honest sex. Then why had he made the slip? Did he want her love?

"Judd." Brenda Sue walked in with that nonchalant attitude that irritated the hell out of him. The woman didn't know what privacy meant. "Oh." She paused for a brief second when she spotted him. "I didn't know if you were in here or not, but Harland's been looking for you. He checked at the house and you weren't there, and he waited last night for you to come home, and finally gave up. I asked him what was so important but he wouldn't say. He keeps things pretty close to his chest, if you know what I mean. You know he's just a tad too serious and grouchy for me, but then most men are like that and…"

He held up a hand and she actually stopped running off at the mouth. "Gave up on taking a breath, huh?"

"Well…" She fidgeted in a self-conscious way he'd never seen before. Brenda Sue never seemed ill at ease. "Monty says my talking doesn't bother him and I have to be, well, myself. I feel awkward when I have to think about what I'm saying. That's just not me, so if people don't like it, they can stuff it. Oh…" She quickly backpedaled. "I don't mean you. Heavens, no. You were actually nice to me and I'll really try not to be annoying when you're around."

It wasn't working.

"But Monty likes me the way I am. No man has ever said that to me before and he was really serious. Sometimes you can't tell, but—"

"Monty Crabtree who works here?" Judd interrupted, to save his sanity. In his forties, Monty was a quiet, hardworking man who was a cowboy to the core. Conversing was not his forte. He preferred peace and quiet. The thought of Monty and Brenda Sue as a couple was almost comical. Or maybe they were made for each other. What did Judd know?

"Yeah. His mother lives down the road from my parents. I had a flat in front of her house about two weeks ago and Monty fixed it. He was so nice. Men usually are jerks, but he actually listens to what I'm saying. I asked if I was getting on his nerves and he said the sweetest thing. He said I could never get on his nerves. Isn't that adorable?"

"Yep." Judd was all choked up. "Tell Harland I want to see him—now."

"Oh." She seemed genuinely upset that he didn't want to hear about Monty. And just to make sure she thought he was his normal grouchy self, Judd added, "And don't distract Monty from his work."

She winked, all bubbly and happy. "You got it. I'll go and find Harland. Who knows, I might see Monty. You wouldn't mind that, would you? I mean, I wouldn't be interfering or anything in what he was—"

"Get Harland!" Judd shouted.

She cleared the doorway in a split second.

He leaned back in his chair, not able to get last night out of his head. His love—that's all Caitlyn wanted. Why couldn't he give her that? She'd said it started with caring. He took care of Whiskey Red for her, not letting anyone touch the horse but him. What did that say?

It said he was a flawed individual incapable of accepting the greatest gift of all—love. Was that bull? Cait had said everyone was capable of love. For the first time in his life Judd wanted to experience the emotion, to give Caitlyn everything she wanted. But just like fourteen years ago, he was the one standing in the way of their happiness. Could he continue to live like this?

A tap at the door interrupted his thoughts.

"Come in," he called.

Harland stepped in and closed the door. "Good morning, Judd."

"Morning."

The foreman took a seat in front of Judd's desk. "The Belle woman is a problem again."

"Walker contacted me yesterday about Caitlyn and the calf." He leaned forward slightly, watching Harland's face.

"Good." The man nodded. "Something has to be done. The woman pulled a gun on us."

"Walker and I talked to Caitlyn. She said you threatened to kill the calf."

"Come on, Judd. You're not going to believe that, are you?" Harland moved awkwardly in his chair, the only sign he might be nervous.

"I just know one of my prize heifers was found miles from the corral she was supposed to be in. How did that happen?"

"One of the boys must have left the gate open for a second while he was feeding. As soon as I realized she was gone, we tracked her. But we were too late."

Judd rested his forearms on the desk, his eyes holding Harland's. "That's a damn big loss and I'm not happy about this situation."

"I know. I'll have a talk with the boys."

"*I'll* talk to the boys." His words were clipped. Harland stood. "If that's what you want."

Judd hated his condescending tone. "Gather them at the bunkhouse in ten minutes."

"Okay. Afterward, do you want me to go over and pick up the calf?"

Judd could see Harland was looking forward to the task. "No. Miss Belle is keeping the calf."

"What?"

He lifted an eyebrow. "You have a problem with that?"

"It's your decision." From his voice he might have been saying, "You idiot."

"That's what I thought."

Harland walked out without another word.

Ten minutes later Judd talked to the cowboys and made it clear he wouldn't tolerate sloppy work and the loss of a prize animal. He was angry and he didn't hide it. He wanted to get his point across.

Later he and Ron went over the books, including gas, feed and supplies. Judd was checking every expense of the ranching operation. Every now and then he was distracted, though. *You can love. You just have to allow yourself to.* Caitlyn's words intruded at the oddest times.

Was she right?

THE DROUGHT WAS CAUSING a problem, but another hurricane was forecasted to hit Galveston by the end of the week. The last storm had missed them completely. Cait was hoping for rain.

She put off culling the herd until the bad weather was over. With enough rain, the ranch could survive the hot summer. They spent the day making sure High Five was ready for whatever Mother Nature threw at her.

Later Cait stood in her bedroom and looked out the window toward Southern Cross. She wondered if Judd had talked to Harland, and what kind of excuses he'd gotten for the heifer being so far away from her corral.

No one had come for the calf, but she knew Judd's word was as good as gold. That's the kind of man he was—honest and forthright. She wished he'd allow himself to express all his other good qualities. But wishing was going to give her a big headache.

She wasn't giving up, though, even if she had to use some of Sky's tactics.

Stretching, she realized how tired she was. Dust and sweat coated her skin and there was dirt beneath her fingernails—not sexy, attractive qualities. The responsibility of the ranch was draining her femininity. Was this what her father had meant?

She caught sight of the red dress hanging on the back of her closet door. Grass stains and dirt marred the skirt. She took the garment down and held it to her, dancing around the room. Closing her eyes, she thought of Judd and his strong arms and tempting kisses. All those feminine feelings resurfaced in a flash and she smiled. Oh yeah, she was still alive, and she knew this was what life was all about.

Somehow, some way, she had to convince Judd of that.

CHAPTER NINETEEN

JUDD SPENT THE WEEK investigating the books of Southern Cross. It didn't take him long to find discrepancies. And they all pointed to Harland. After talking to his gas and diesel supplier, Judd found Harland was taking kickbacks from a guy in the office. He always ordered five hundred gallons of fuel, but the company only delivered four. Southern Cross paid for the five and the guy in the office refunded the difference, splitting it with Harland.

Harland was chipping away at the ranch's profits, a fact that angered and frustrated Judd. It was all done under his nose. He had trusted the man like his father had. But Harland didn't have allegiance to anyone but himself and his pocketbook.

Walker had also uncovered damning evidence. Two Southern Cross Brahman heifers had been sold in Oklahoma and one in Louisiana. The buyers still had the receipts, with Harland's signature. The foreman hadn't even tried to cover his tracks.

"Since I don't have a holding facility for prisoners, I contacted the county sheriff. I'll arrest Harland and transport him to the jail. The sheriff is sending a deputy for backup in case there's a problem," Walker said as they sat in Judd's office. "We have enough to put him away for a long time."

"Yeah, but I want to talk to Harland before the deputy gets here." Judd stood and went into the outer office. "Brenda Sue, tell Harland I want to see him."

She looked up from her desk. "What? I don't know where he is. This is a big place and I step in stuff when I go out there. I have new shoes and I don't want to get—"

"I didn't ask for an excuse. I asked for you to find him—now."

"Oh, okay." Brenda Sue got to her feet in a huff. "I can see you're in one of those moods. I don't understand why men are so touchy. You'd think you were the ones with PMS, but oh, no, you get off easy and still most of you act like a bear with a sore head. I'll never understand men and I've given up trying." She was still chattering as she went out the door.

Judd headed back to his office, but swung around again when he heard the door open. Brenda Sue stood there. Damn it! Today wasn't a day to try his patience. He was in a mood to fire everyone on this ranch, including her.

"Now don't lose your temper," she said in a

rush. "Monty was outside and I asked him where Harland was and he said in the bunkhouse. There's no way I'm going in there with all those cowboys, so Monty went to get him. Isn't that sweet?"

When Judd didn't respond, she added, "That's okay, isn't it?"

"He better be here in five minutes." With that, he slammed his office door.

"Calm down, Judd," Walker said.

Judd ran his hands over his face. "I'm just so damn angry. I haven't been this angry since…"

"Since Caitlyn left," Walker finished the sentence.

He sank into his chair. "I forgot you were home at the time."

"Yep. Your father and you were certain she'd come crawling back."

Judd grunted. "I was a fool for listening to my dad."

"Jack had old-fashioned ideas about women." Walker made a steeple with his fingers and Judd could feel his eyes on him. "But I sense you see those ideas for what they are. Rubbish and chauvinistic."

"It's hard to change habits of a lifetime."

"But you and Caitlyn seem to be getting along a little better. I mean, I thought you'd take that calf back come hell or high water. Your father would have."

"Yes, he would, and probably have her arrested, too." Judd drew a long breath. "I'm trying very hard not to be like him."

Walker eyed him observantly. "It's more than that, isn't it?"

A tap at the door prevented Judd from answering, and it was just as well. He didn't have an answer.

"Showtime," Walker said, getting to his feet and moving to Judd's right.

"Come in," Judd called.

Harland walked in and glanced from one man to the other. "Didn't expect to see you here, Walker."

"Didn't expect to be here," he replied.

"Have a seat," Judd said.

Harland eased into a chair, his eyes on his boss. "What's this about?"

Judd pushed a manila folder across the desk. "This will explain everything."

With a frown, Harland stood and picked up the folder. Opening it, he read through the contents and then slammed it onto the desk. "So the jig is up?" he said, his Adam's apple bobbing.

Judd leaned forward, his eyes holding Harland's like a fishhook holds a worm. "You've been stealing from Southern Cross for years."

"Can you blame me?" His face turned beet red in anger. "I repeatedly asked your father for a raise and he repeatedly refused. He said he would deed me land when he died. I worked my ass off for that land, but the bastard lied. He didn't leave me a penny. No one does that to me. No one."

"So you started stealing?" Walker asked.

"You bet." The words came out as a growl. "What better way to get even and stick it to the favorite son. I was finally getting the money I deserved. If that Belle woman hadn't interfered, you never would have found out."

"You've been sabotaging High Five, haven't you?" Judd asked.

"That woman needs to be put in her place. Your father would have made sure of that. High Five would have been a part of Southern Cross by now, but you kowtow to the bitch. Your father must be turning over in his grave."

Judd stood, his hands clenched. He wanted to jump across the desk and strangle the man, or reach for the Colt .45 in the bottom drawer and show Harland who was boss. But he did neither of those things. Mainly because he knew it was exactly what his father would have done. Judd was a better man than that.

Walker stepped forward. "Albert Harland, you're under arrest for—"

"You're having me arrested?" Harland glared at Judd.

"You've stolen thousands of dollars. Did you

think I was just going to let that slide?" He un-clenched his hands as some of the tension left him. "Since you're so big on my father's attri-butes, you should know he would have blown your brains out. Be grateful I'm letting the justice system take care of you."

"You bastard," Harland spat. "You'll pay for this. That bitch will, too."

Before he or Walker could gauge his intent, Harland ran from the room, slamming the door in their faces to slow them down. Walker drew the gun from his belt holster and yanked opened the door. Judd was right behind him.

"What's happening?" Brenda Sue asked.

Neither responded as they made a dash for the front door. Monty stood outside like a lovesick fool.

"Where's Harland?" Judd demanded.

"He ran for the stables."

Judd and Walker hurried there, but Harland was nowhere in sight. Then, Chuck walked up from the tack room.

"Have you seen Harland?" Judd asked.

"He just rode out of here like the devil was after him."

"Which way did he go?"

Chuck pointed toward the High Five.

"Damn it!"

"Was he alone?" Walker asked.

"No," Chuck replied. "Those new cowboys, Ernie and Ray, were with him."

"Thanks, Chuck." Judd moved a short distance away to speak to Walker.

"What do you think?" The constable slid his gun back into his holster.

"I think he's gone after Caitlyn." The mere thought made Judd's stomach tighten. He reached for the cell phone hooked on his belt, and punched out High Five's number.

Etta answered.

"Etta, this is Judd Calhoun. Is Caitlyn there?"

"Heavens, no. She left early to take care of everything before that hurricane blows through here."

He'd almost forgotten about the hurricane. "Do you know where she went?"

"No, but Maddie might."

"May I speak to her?"

"Who?"

Judd drew a patient breath. "Maddie."

"Oh. Okay."

A second later she was on the line. "Maddie, this is Judd. Do you know what part of the ranch Caitlyn is on?"

"Oh, hi, Judd. Cait left early with Cooper and Rufus, and I have no idea where she went. She did mention something about checking a windmill and all water sources."

"Thanks, Maddie."

"Is something wrong?"

"No. I just need to find Cait." He clicked off and shouted to Chuck, "Get my horse and a horse for Walker—pronto."

Walker was on his cell and turned to Judd. "I was talking to the sheriff to apprise him of the situation. I assume we're going after Harland."

"You got it. We have to reach Caitlyn before he does."

CAIT DISMOUNTED at the windmill, relieved to discover everything was working fine. She glanced south and could see dark clouds rolling in. The area was expecting high winds and heavy rain, and from the looks of the sky she knew the storm would be here soon. Time to head back to the ranch to make sure Gran and everyone were safe.

As she turned she saw smoke coming from the west. It seemed to be in the location of her hay fields. Could they be on fire? She swung back toward Jaz and froze. Harland and two cowboys had come up on horseback. One of the cowboys reached for Jaz's reins and pulled her away.

Cait's heart kicked against her ribs. This was trouble. Without her rifle, she had no way to defend herself against three men, except maybe to bluff her way out of whatever Harland had in mind.

"The hurricane is on its way, so we better get out of the weather," she said, playing it cool.

"You're not going anywhere, Miss Belle," Harland replied in an icy tone. "It's payback day for all the times you stuck your nose in my business. You're the reason my lucrative job is gone, and you're going to pay."

Judd had fired him? At the evil glint in Harland's eyes, fear like she'd never known before inched up her spine and she took a step backward. The man was going to kill her.

She knew that as well as she knew her own name.

Harland dismounted, as did one of the cowboys. She quickly weighed her options and realized she had only one—the windmill. Turning swiftly, she sprinted for the ladder and began to climb.

"Get her," Harland shouted.

The cowboy was right behind her. He grabbed her boot, but she held on tight and kicked back with her other foot. Her boot heel connected with his face.

"Bitch," he shouted, clutching his cheek with one hand. Blood oozed through his fingers.

"Get her," Harland shouted again, from below. "Yank her off there."

She didn't pause to see what the guy was doing; she climbed higher. The wind picked up and she felt the tower sway. Her hat blew off and she held on with all her might. But what good was that if the windmill went down? *Oh, God.* She needed help.

There was no one out here, though, and Harland knew that. He was going to make sure she died here.

JUDD GALLOPED at breakneck speed toward the smoke on the High Five ranch. Walker was right behind. They came into the clearing of the hay fields, noting the scorched, charred ground. Cooper and Rufus were fighting the flames with horse blankets, trying to beat them out.

"Call the volunteer fire department," Judd yelled to Walker.

Cooper heard him. "I already did. They're on the way."

At that moment two fire trucks and a number of firefighters roared onto the site. The men immediately went to work, fighting the conflagration and the rising wind. Judd hoped the rain wasn't far behind.

"Where's Caitlyn?" he yelled.

Cooper paused from beating at the blaze. "She went to check the windmill."

Judd swung his horse in that direction, as did Walker. He knew Caitlyn didn't have a lot of time. After galloping into the pasture, they pulled up short. Judd saw Caitlyn climbing the shaky windmill, a cowboy right behind her. Harland and another cowboy stood on the ground, watching.

Judd drew his rifle from the saddle scabbard and Walker drew his gun. They jumped off their horses at the same time.

Walker took care of Harland and the cowboy. Judd pointed his rifle at the man on the windmill. "Come down," he shouted against the wind, "or I'm going to shoot you off of there."

The man stopped climbing.

"Now!" Judd shouted again.

Slowly the cowboy began to descend. Walker had handcuffed Harland and trained his gun on the two men. A deputy drove up just then and Walker started talking to him, but Judd's eyes were on Caitlyn at the top of the swaying windmill. As the wind tugged at it, she bent her head, her hands clamped tight around the ladder.

A number of options ran through Judd's mind, but none of them seemed right. If he climbed up, the tower might fall with his weight. That was a sure death sentence—for both of them.

He laid his rifle on the ground and cupped his hands around his mouth. "Caitlyn, you have to jump. I'll catch you. Trust me."

Cait heard Judd. *He wanted her to jump! To trust him.* Was he insane? The wind was fierce and she didn't know how much longer the windmill could withstand it. She couldn't jump, though. She was frightened out of her mind.

"Come on, Caitie. We don't have a lot of time. Just push back with your boots and I'll catch you. Trust me, Caitie. I won't let you down this time. Let go and push back…."

That caring, coaxing tone did the trick. The windmill rocked and she knew she had to trust Judd as she'd never trusted anyone in her life. She closed her eyes, said a prayer and then pried her clammy fingers from the rung and pushed out with her feet. The air left her lungs as her body plunged through open space. She heard a scream and realized it was her.

She seemed to lose consciousness for a second and the next thing she knew, strong arms had snatched her from the air. Together, she and her savior tumbled backward. But she was safe on the ground—in Judd's arms.

His hands moved over her body. "Are you okay?"

She drew a breath that scorched her lungs, and then another. "Y-yes. I think."

Walker rushed over. "Wow, Caitlyn, I didn't know you could fly."

She made a face at him and staggered to her feet. Judd was there to steady her, and she leaned on him.

"We have Harland and his boys handcuffed and

in the deputy's car," Walker said. "I'm going back
to get my car and I'll meet you at the sheriff's office."

By then the deputy had joined them. "You need
to sign papers," he said, looking toward the sky.
"And we better get out of here. Heavy rain is on
the way and that windmill is not too steady."

They moved away from the shaky structure.
"I'll make sure Caitlyn is okay and then I'll follow
you," Judd stated.

The deputy got in his car and drove away. Walker
hightailed it on horseback to the Southern Cross.

Judd looked at Caitlyn's pale face. "Are you
sure you're okay?"

She tilted her head. "Well, Judd Calhoun, you
keep asking me that and I'm going to start
thinking you care." As she said the words, rain-
drops pelted their faces.

"We'd better take cover," Judd said, grabbing
Baron's and Jaz's reins. He led them into a gully,
away from the windmill and trees. He yanked a
slicker from his saddlebag. Spreading the rain gear
over their heads, he hunkered down with Caitlyn
to wait out the worst of the storm.

"Wouldn't it be better to make a run for the
ranch?" she asked.

"It's too dangerous now with the wind, light-
ning and rain. Hopefully it will be over soon."

Under the plastic covering, they seemed to be

encased in their own private world. The rain beat down and the wind tugged at them fiercely. They held tight to the slicker, which the wind kept threatening to blow away.

Suddenly they heard a loud crash. "The windmill," Caitlyn muttered, grateful she wasn't still on it. The slashing rain kept battering them, but she wasn't afraid. She had Judd.

Under the slicker she smelled rain, sweat and sandalwood. And Judd. He filled every corner of her mind.

"I wouldn't have jumped for anyone else," she murmured. "I trusted you."

He turned his head and she stared into the dark depths of his eyes. "That's what love is," she added. "Trusting another person completely." She unsnapped her shirt, took his hand and placed it over her heart. "Can you feel it?"

His eyes darkened. "Caitlyn—"

"Don't say you don't know what love is. All you have to do is follow the instructions you gave me a moment ago. Let go, open up your heart and trust me. *Trust* me."

His hand moved over her breast and his eyes held hers. Slowly he dipped his head and his lips took hers hungrily. Neither held anything back. The world, the storm, faded away as their hands and lips found a way to ease the pain of yesterday.

Distracted, they lost their grip on the slicker and the wind took it. "Oh," she cried as she tried to catch it, to no avail. Judd pulled her back into his arms and she buried her face in the warmth of his neck. The rain showed no mercy, drenching them both, but then suddenly eased off again. Even the wind dropped. The gully was filling up with water, and Judd helped her to her feet.

Cait stared at the crushed windmill and defeat washed over her as hard as the rain had. It was going to cost a lot to get it back up and running.

"We can make it home now," Judd said, brushing rain from her face.

She wanted to stay in this moment, in this time. He hadn't said he loved her, but he hadn't denied it, either. That was enough for now.

But thoughts of the ranch and her responsibilities came rushing back. She reached for Jaz's reins. "I saw smoke earlier. Do you know what that was?"

Judd seemed to take a long time to answer. "Your hay fields were on fire and I'm pretty sure Harland and his boys set it." Then he told her all he'd learned about the foreman.

She swallowed hard. "I think he was going to kill me."

"No doubt. He blamed you that I found out about his illegal activities."

"Is that why you came looking for me?"

"Yes. When he realized he was going to be arrested, he said he'd make you pay."

She swung into the saddle with a squeaky wet sound. She was soaked, as was the saddle and her horse. "I have to get home to check on my family."

"I'll come with you," Judd called, and jumped onto Baron. Together they galloped toward High Five. As they came over a ridge, Cait pulled up. Puffs of smoke could be seen coming from the house.

"Oh, no!" She kneed Jaz and was off again like a rocket. She had to find out if Gran, Maddie and Etta were okay.

Jaz covered the wet ground with amazing speed. As they reached the barnyard, Cait leaped off and made a dash for the smoldering house.

Please let them be okay, she prayed.

"Cait!"

She swung around at the sound of Maddie's voice, and saw her, Coop and Rufus standing under the eave of the barn. Gran wasn't with them. Cait's heart sank to the pit of her stomach.

She ran to Maddie, her breath catching. "Where's Gran?" she cried anxiously. "Tell me where she is!"

Maddie put an arm around her and Cait realized her sister was as wet as she was. "It's okay. Gran is at Etta's lying down. She's fine, but a little shaken up, as we all are."

Cait glanced toward the puffs of smoke still coming from the house. "How bad is it?"

"The parlor and two bedrooms sustained damage."

Cait swallowed the constriction in her throat. "How did this happen?"

"Etta and I were working in the kitchen and we smelled smoke. I went into the parlor and saw the blaze at the windows. It traveled to the second floor before Cooper and I could get it out with water hoses."

"But how did it start?"

Coop stepped forward, his face etched in anger. "I was getting ready to go check the rolls of hay to make sure they were secure, and saw Harland and two cowboys ride away. I heard Maddie scream, and I ran to the house. While she got Miss Dorie and Etta out, I grabbed the hoses to extinguish the fire."

"Thank you, Coop."

"I wish I could have saved more. I smelled gasoline and knew that bastard had torched the place."

"And the hay fields?" Cait asked, but she already knew.

Coop removed his wet hat and studied it for a moment. "As we finished putting out the fire at the house, I saw the smoke coming from the hay fields. I told Maddie to call the fire department, and Ru and I got there as fast as we could. But it was too late. The dry grasses and the wind were against us. I'm sorry, Cait. We lost it all."

She took a deep breath and wanted to burst into tears. All her hard work and it was gone. High Five was done. There was no way she could recover from this.

She collected herself quickly. She wouldn't cry. At that moment she looked up and saw that half the tin roof on the barn had been blown away. The tears weren't far away, but the thought of the baby calf saved her.

"Is Solomon okay?"

"Yes." Maddie squeezed her shoulder. "He's in there bumping his head, wanting milk. I'll feed him in a little bit."

Cooper tensed, and out of her peripheral vision Cait saw Judd walk up.

"I'm sorry, Caitlyn," he said.

She turned to face him, and all that love and warmth she'd felt earlier seemed to disappear. She was spent and empty.

"We won't have to wait for six months," she said in a voice she didn't recognize. "Harland has beaten me and High Five is finished. You were right—I was fighting a losing battle."

He took a step forward. "Cait…"

"Please leave. I'll get with you later about the details. I can't handle any more right now."

"Cait…"

Cooper stepped in front of her. "You heard the lady. It's time for you to go."

The two men, the same height and weight, faced off. "I don't want to fight with you, Cooper."

"Then leave."

Judd glanced at Cait. "Is this your kind of trust?"

She couldn't answer. Her whole body was frozen in abject misery. She dropped her gaze and he walked to his horse and rode away.

And out of her life for good.

CHAPTER TWENTY

CAITLYN TURNED and walked into the barn. Maddie and Cooper were right behind her.

"Please," she said over her shoulder, "I need some time alone."

"Cait…"

She faced her sister. "Please, give me a moment."

Maddie hesitated. "Okay. I'll go check on Gran."

"Tell her I'll be there in a minute."

Maddie nodded.

With methodical movements, Cait went into the supply room, which still had a roof, and mixed milk for Solomon. It was mundane work and she needed that. She carried the bottle to the stall and opened the gate. Solomon trotted to her, eager for food. He bumped his head against her leg and she sank into the straw and held the milk out to him. As he grabbed the nipple, she gripped the bottle tightly because she knew he'd jerk it out of her hand.

He drank the contents in no time and curled up

beside her, satisfied. She wished her problems could be solved so easily. Setting the bottle aside, she drew up her knees and wrapped her arms around them. She glanced toward the end of the barn and the gray sky peeping through the gaping holes of the torn-off tin. Destruction was all around her. But life was, too. Solomon was new life, a new beginning.

She stared at that patch of sky and wondered if her father was looking down and saying those words she hated to hear. *I told you so.* Maybe he was right. Ranching wasn't women's work.

The odds had always been against her, but she'd been too stubborn to see that. Now she had to admit defeat and say goodbye to her beloved High Five. Uninvited tears slid from her eyes. She slapped them away, but more followed. She wasn't sure what she was crying about—losing High Five or losing Judd. Again.

There was no way they'd survive this. Their love wasn't meant to be, and she had to accept that and move on. She took some solace in the thought of Judd rebuilding High Five. It would prosper like in the olden days.

But she wouldn't be here.

More tears followed and she didn't try to stop them. She was a woman, and damn it, women cried.

After a moment she drew a shaky breath.

Now she had to find the strength to look at the damages to the house. And she had to find the strength to tell Gran. That was her responsibility.

Cait got to her feet and headed for the house, her boots sinking into the sodden ground. As she opened the door, lingering traces of smoke filled her lungs and nausea churned in her stomach. One wall in the parlor was scorched and the velvet drapes were gone. The fire had spread up the wall to the bedrooms, and those walls were burned, too. They would have to be ripped out and replaced. That would take money—dollars she didn't have.

She did have insurance, but it would take weeks before she received funds. Where would they live in the meantime?

Nothing else was insured. She couldn't afford it. That meant High Five would not be able to recover from the losses.

Giving up wasn't easy, but this was destruction Cait couldn't beat. Stoically, she marched to her bedroom, which miraculously hadn't been touched, and stripped off her wet clothes. Her wet braid was heavy, so she undid it and towel dried her hair. After that she put on clean, dry clothes and went downstairs and out the door to talk to Gran.

The cabin was small, with a combination

kitchen, dining room and living area, along with two bedrooms and a bath. When Cait had the strength, she'd talk to Judd about letting Etta and Rufus stay here.

In the living room, she hugged Etta.

"Lordy, Lordy, it's awful. Just awful," the housekeeper moaned.

"How's Gran?"

"She's resting." Etta wiped away a tear. "Maddie's with her." The woman gave Cait a push toward a bedroom. "You better go in there. She's worried about you."

Caitlyn walked into the room. Maddie sat cross-legged on the bed, talking to Gran, who was propped up with fluffy pillows.

"Hi, Gran," Cait said as she sat beside her. She looked so pale with her white hair hanging around her face. Cait felt a catch in her throat.

Dorie reached for her and hugged her tightly. "My baby, I've been so worried."

"I got caught in the storm, so I had to wait it out." Cait drew back and tucked loose strands of black hair behind her ears. "I got a little wet, but I'm fine."

"I'll go help Etta with supper," Maddie said, sliding off the bed.

Gran picked up Cait's cold hand. "Don't look so worried, my baby."

She tried to wipe her feelings from her face, but couldn't—not even for her grandmother. "I'll try," she made herself say.

"How's the house?" Dorie asked.

"It's going to need a lot of repairs." She didn't lie. The time for that was over.

"I figured," Gran said, surprising her.

It must have shown on her face, because Gran added, "I know you girls think I'm a senile old woman living in the past."

"Oh, Gran." Cait squeezed her hand.

"It's okay, because most of the time I am. But I know what's going on, Caitlyn."

Gran never called her that unless she was serious, so Cait listened closely. "What are you talking about?"

The old woman pushed herself up against the pillows. "I know Dane sold Judd our oil and gas royalties."

"What?" She had her full attention now.

"Dane told me what he had to do. It was his only way out of all his gambling debts." Gran sighed. "I spoiled him terribly and I'm afraid he never learned to live within his means. He had too many bad habits that I ignored because I loved him."

Cait was speechless, so she just kept listening.

Gran twisted her hands together. "He assured

me that everything would work out and that he had made the right decision for you, Maddie and Sky."

"Selling our means of livelihood was the right decision?" The words came out angry, but Cait couldn't stop them.

Gran patted her hands. "Don't fret, child. I know Judd will be buying High Five now. I've resigned myself to that. Your father wanted you to have a life, and now maybe you can find the one you want."

"My life has always been here."

"I think that was to defy your father." Gran looked into her eyes. "What do you really want, baby?"

Judd had asked her the same thing.

Instead of answering, she burst into tears. Gran held her as if she were six years old. "Don't cry, baby, and don't worry about me. I'm a strong old woman and I've survived worse. You do what you have to."

Cait brushed away tears—once she started crying she couldn't seem to stop. "I'm not sure what that is yet. But High Five has received a death blow. I'm not certain what to do next."

Her grandmother stroked her cheek. "You'll know, baby."

Cait stood and stared at her. "What else do you know, Gran?"

"Everything," she replied with a secret smile.

"Everything?"

"That's one good thing about spoiling my son. He told me everything."

"You mean…" Cait wasn't sure how to finish the sentence without betraying Maddie or Sky.

"Yes, I know, Maddie has had a fight with cancer and won, but now she won't be able to have children. I also know about Kira. Dane gave me a photo that I'm very proud of. I wish I could say the same about my granddaughters keeping secrets. But I promised Dane I would let them tell me. Sometimes that promise was hard to keep."

Her grandmother was stronger than they had ever given her credit for, and Cait resolved never to keep anything from her again.

Maddie walked in. "Would you like to get up, Gran?"

Dorie swung her feet over the side of the bed. "Yes, I would. I'm ready to handle whatever comes next."

"And that means you," Cait whispered to her sister.

Maddie frowned, not understanding.

"She knows—*everything*." Cait emphasized the last word.

"Oh." Realization dawned in Maddie's blue eyes.

Cait walked out, leaving them to talk. Maybe now they could come together as a family without secrets.

THE NEXT FEW DAYS passed in a blur, but Cait kept busy assessing all the damages to High Five, which were extensive. Cooper was optimistic that they could regroup and overcome. Cait wasn't.

The sheriff called and she went to his office to file more charges against Harland. That gave her some satisfaction.

By the end of the week, Coop and Rufus had a new roof on the barn. She called a man to get an estimate on repairing the windmill. The rest of the time they worked on the house, trying to eradicate the smoke smell and pull off the burned wood. It was a monumental task, but there was something cathartic about toiling until you were so exhausted you fell instantly asleep.

All the time they were working she kept thinking it was useless. They were wasting time and resources. Soon Judd would make an offer for High Five, as he'd promised her father. He'd keep his word, so it was only a matter of time.

But they went on working.

Gran stayed at Etta's, and Cait and Maddie moved into the bunkhouse with Cooper. The arrangement worked well and it kept them on the ranch—for now.

Cait received the estimate for the windmill and the cost of repairing the house. Her eyes bulged at the figures. The insurance adjuster looked at the house and took the estimate, saying he'd be in touch. She had no idea when that would be. She needed the money right away, and told the man that.

Mr. Bardwell had stopped buying sand and gravel because the pits were too wet. He said he'd try again in a month or so, but that would be too late.

She thought of selling the herd, but that was just putting off the inevitable. At the end of the second week she called Judd. Brenda Sue answered.

"Brenda Sue, this is Caitlyn. May I please speak to Judd?"

"He's not here and I don't know where he is. He pretty much does what he wants and, believe me, I don't interfere. You know how men are, but then you may not. You've always been sorta—"

"I'd like to make an appointment to see him." Cait cut her off, trying not to scream.

"I don't make his appointments. He's funny about that, too. You'll have to call back or whatever. I've got to go. I've got things to do and Judd doesn't like me talking on the phone. Did I tell you I have a boyfriend? His name is Monty and…"

Cait gritted her teeth and shut out whatever Brenda Sue was rattling on about. "Tell him I'll be there at ten in the morning to discuss High Five. You can give him a message, right?"

"Of course I can, and that's just like you,

Caitlyn. You always have to have your way. That's why you're still single and—"

"Give him the message," she yelled, and slammed the phone down.

Cait went into her office, which was still usable, and took several deep breaths. Then she sat down and made out a list of points she wanted to negotiate with Judd. She would like for Etta, Rufus and Cooper to be allowed to stay on the property. She, Maddie and Gran hadn't made plans yet. They would decide at the end.

At the bottom she scribbled "I love you. Why wasn't that enough?"

Maddie rushed in, her cell in her hand. She shoved it at Cait. "Sky's on the line."

"Hey, sis, where are you?" Cait asked.

"In this hick town in Tennessee."

"I would tell you to come home, but we don't have too much of a home at the moment. We just about got out all the smoke smell, though."

"Maddie told me. I'm sorry, Cait. I know how hard you've worked."

"Thanks. I guess it wasn't meant to be."

"You sound resigned to the whole thing."

She wasn't. She was dying a little inside, but no one would ever know that.

"Gran's okay with it, so that makes it better for me."

"Speaking of Gran, I hear we haven't kept a thing from her."

"Nope, and I suggest you call her as soon as possible."

"I will, and Cait? Whatever you decide is fine with me."

"Really? Wouldn't you rather have the money?"

"Of course, but you're my sister and I love you and want…" Her voice trailed away.

"Is 'bitchy' getting soft?"

"Not on your life, sister dear."

"I didn't think so." Cait laughed, and it felt good to talk to her sister. "Call Gran," she shouted before clicking off.

"She sounds great, doesn't she?" Maddie asked.

"Yeah. She's a survivor."

"Just like you and me," Maddie stated. "We're going to make it."

"We sure are." Cait stood. "Now let's go make Cooper nervous."

Maddie grinned. "He does get rattled when we walk around in nothing but a towel."

"Mmm. I guess we need to be more respectful of his privacy."

"Maybe." Maddie made a face. "But then we'd have no fun."

They giggled and went out the door arm in arm.

JUDD SAT IN HIS STUDY staring at a glass of bourbon, but all he could see was Caitlyn's face. He couldn't seem to get it out of his head.

Please leave. I'll get with you later about the details. I can't handle any more right now.

Why couldn't she trust him not to hurt her again? But of course, she couldn't recover from the enormous loss, and he had to buy High Five. He'd promised Dane. Judd couldn't go back on his word.

That would destroy all the progress they'd made in the last few months.

Could he hurt her that way?

So many times she'd tried to tell him about love, and each time he'd resisted.

Love starts by caring.

Well, he cared. When she was on that windmill, he knew if she fell and died, life wouldn't be worth living, just as it hadn't been for the past fourteen years. That was a wad of truth to swallow.

Love is a special connection between two people.

They'd certainly had that from day one, even fourteen years ago. He was just too pigheaded to see it or to admit it.

Let go, open your heart and trust me. Trust *me.* She'd trusted him on the windmill, and she probably had always trusted him.

Love is something you feel in the heart.

When she saw her family home in ruins, the pain

in her eyes had cut through his gut. He'd wanted to take that pain away, but she'd told him to leave.

Trust me.

"Judd," Brenda Sue called a moment before opening the door.

He clenched his jaw at this intrusion.

"Oh, good, you're here," the secretary said. "I didn't know if you were back or not, and I was leaving for the day. I was going to write you a message, but now I can just tell you. Caitlyn called and wanted to make an appointment to see you. I told her I didn't make your appointments and she got huffy. You know how Caitlyn is. She said to tell you she'd be here at ten in the morning to discuss High Five. You know, I heard there was a lot of damage there and—"

He held up a hand to stop the endless chatter. "Call her back and tell her I have appointments in Austin tomorrow. I'll meet with her later."

Brenda Sue pointed to his phone. "Why don't *you* call her?"

He lifted an eyebrow. "And what do I pay you for?"

"Oh, okay, but Caitlyn's going to bite my head off. I'd just as soon not go another round with her if you know what I mean. But if it's my job I guess I have no choice."

Judd leaned back in his chair. "Try not to criticize. That might help. Just give her the message and don't elaborate on anything else. It's that simple."

Brenda Sue scrunched up her nose. "I'll try to be short and brief. I better hurry. I promised to meet Monty and I don't want to be late. It's our—"

"Short and brief," he reminded her, and she hurried out the door.

He flipped through his Rolodex for Frank's number. Before talking to Caitlyn, Judd had to know his legal rights concerning High Five.

Could he take everything she loved?

CAITLYN WAS MIFFED when she got the call from Brenda Sue. She tried to question her, but the blasted woman hung up on her. Was Judd avoiding her? They had to talk. There were no ifs, ands or buts about it.

After the fire, she hadn't been too nice to him. She'd been in shock, but now they had to find a way to communicate. And she had to find a way to let go. Of High Five.

And Judd.

In the late afternoon, Chance drove in with the bed of his truck filled with lumber and building supplies. She and Maddie ran out to greet him.

After hugs, Cait asked, "Are you going into construction?"

"Nope." He removed his hat and bowed from the

waist. "I am at your service, ma'am, to help rebuild the house."

"But I don't have any money to pay you. I'm waiting on the insurance money."

"Miss Dorie never asked for money all the times I ate at her table, so I'm just repaying High Five's hospitality."

"Chance Hardin, you're an angel."

"I'll get Cooper so he can help you unload this," Maddie said.

Chance grinned. "I'd appreciate it." As Maddie walked away, he turned to Cait. "Could I talk to you for a sec?"

"Sure." He sounded serious and she wondered what this was about.

He removed his hat and slicked back his dark hair in a nervous gesture. "I've been offered a job—a really good job. I could stay in one place and not be on the road so much. Also, I would be around to help Etta and Rufus when they need it."

"So the job is in High Cotton?"

"Yeah." He shifted from one booted foot to the other and she was taken aback by his nervousness. He looked up. "Judd offered me the foreman's job at Southern Cross."

"So?" She couldn't make the connection. After Harland, she knew Judd would be looking for someone. Chance had worked on Southern Cross for a lot of years before taking off for the oil fields. He and Judd had remained good friends.

"Well, I know there's a lot of tension between the two families and—"

She pinched his arm. "Take the job. Etta would love to have you close." Cait didn't go into High Five's shaky future. That wouldn't be resolved until she talked to Judd, and she had no idea when that would be. But it gave her comfort to know that Chance might also be looking after High Five and its future.

For the next couple of days, Chance, Cooper and Rufus worked on repairing the house. She and Maddie helped when they could. But Cait's thoughts remained centered on Judd. Why hadn't he called? Brenda Sue had said he'd be in touch, yet so far she'd heard nothing. That left her in limbo. That left her angry. That left her testing her patience.

But she waited.

CHAPTER TWENTY-ONE

SOLOMON WAS GETTING so big that she and Maddie had a hard time controlling him. One butt could knock them for a loop. They were now giving him small amounts of sweet feed, which added to his weight. The calf was always greedy, wanting more.

"I don't think we're ever going to fill him up!" Maddie said as she closed the gate.

"He's a growing boy." Cait laughed as Solomon butted the slats. She banged her fist against the railing. "Stop." Suddenly, over the calf's bleating and shuffling, they heard the thunder of hooves. The sisters looked at each other in puzzlement. The guys were working on the house, so it couldn't be one of them. Before they could take a step to investigate, Whiskey Red galloped into the barn.

"Oh, my God," Cait cried, running to the horse and throwing her arms around her neck. "She must have gotten away." Stroking Red, she added, "I have to take her back." As she thought about it, she knew this was the perfect opportunity to see Judd. Time to face him and sort out the future. He wasn't avoiding her any longer.

She led Red to her stall and turned to Maddie. "Please feed her. I have to see Judd."

"Okay," her sister replied, a bit mystified.

Cait ran to her truck, shoved it into gear and drove steadily toward the Southern Cross. She stopped on the circular drive. Jumping out, she ran for the front door and tapped the brass knocker. No response. She opened the door and went inside, straight to Judd's study. He wasn't there. She went into the hallway and ran into Renee.

"Oh. I didn't realize we had company." The woman smiled at her.

She didn't return the smile. "I'm looking for Judd."

Renee shrugged. "He's on the ranch somewhere, seeing to all the damages the hurricane caused."

"Was the loss substantial?"

"Just minor stuff, but Judd seems to need to work twelve hour days."

"Oh." Cait knew the feeling. She'd worked so hard to save High Five and it was all for nothing. Her eyes focused on the Persian rug in the foyer and it reminded her of the day when Judd had told her about the sale of the royalties.

"Renee, how much did Judd pay for High Five's

royalties?" She'd never asked that question and she suddenly needed to know.

Renee didn't even pause before answering. "Over half a million."

OhmyGod! Cait had never imagined. All this time she'd thought Judd had finagled her father into selling, but with a gambling debt that large her dad really had had no choice. The Belle family was lucky Judd had bought the royalties. It had saved them from a worse fate.

"Would you please tell Judd..." Her voice trailed off as he strolled down the hall.

"I think you can tell him yourself, my dear." Renee patted her son's arm and disappeared out the door.

Judd looked tired, but it didn't diminish his appeal. "You wanted to see me?" he asked, walking into his study.

"Yes." She clenched her hands at his gruff expression. "I wanted to let you know Red is at my place, in case you were looking for her."

"I'm not," he replied, sinking into his chair and shuffling through papers on his desk.

That shook her. What did he mean? "Well, somehow she got loose and—"

"She didn't get loose." He leaned back in his chair, his eyes holding hers. "I let her go."

That made no sense at all. "Why?"

"She's your horse, not mine."

"You bought her."

"Out of spite." He jammed both hands through his dark hair. "You see, Caitlyn, I find it very hard taking things you love."

That almost blew her out of her boots. "Still..." That was all she could say. Warm feelings suffused her whole body and she couldn't think.

"Consider it a wedding gift."

Her eyes narrowed on his. "Excuse me?"

He leaned forward, his expression keeping her from jumping for joy. Tapping a document on his desk, he added, "I talked to Frank about the codicil. He said it was my choice whether to invoke it or not, so I've thought long and hard about this." He took a breath. "I've decided against taking High Five, for the reason I've already told you. But I have a solution for its future. As my wife you will own half of all my holdings, including the gas and oil royalties. Your half will go back into High Five, the other half will go toward the amount I paid for them. High Five will have funds to recoup."

She could hardly believe her ears. "Is this a marriage proposal?"

Without a flicker of emotion, he answered, "Yes."

Joy wasn't the first thing she felt. Anger was. After all their talks, he hadn't changed. The cold proposal was the same as it had been fourteen years ago—without love. She would not sacrifice her pride, her dignity for anything else.

She walked closer to his desk. "The answer is no."

"What?" He was clearly shocked.

"Are you hard of hearing?"

His lips twitched. "No."

She stared directly at him. "You know my bottom line. It's the same as it was the last time you proposed. Without love we have nothing, and until you can open your heart and accept what you're really feeling, there will be no marriage—not even to save High Five."

He looked stunned.

"You once asked me what I really wanted. I want you. I want your love, not a business deal." She swung toward the door. "You have until midnight to make your decision." She walked out as fear edged its way into her heart.

It was all or nothing. What would Judd do?

JUDD STARED AFTER HER in complete misery. But what had he really been expecting? That she would be grateful...? He ran both hands over his face. For days all he could think about was their situation, and he'd thought he'd found a solution. It was easy for him—he wouldn't have to sacrifice his heart and his soul. He'd protected that part of himself for so long, and was still doing it.

He drew a heavy breath. *Open your heart.* Cait didn't realize how hard that was for him. But if he wanted her... *I want your love, not a business deal.*

This time, could he give her what she asked for?

His mother breezed in. "What did Caitlyn want?"

"My soul."

Renee placed her hands on her hips. "Well, wrap it up with a pretty red bow and give it to her."

"You have a warped sense of humor."

"Son, it's not humor. It's desperation."

He shook his head. "What are you talking about?"

"Why do you think I gave that ridiculous ball?" She didn't give him a chance to respond. "I wanted you and Caitlyn to remember how happy and in love you were at your engagement party. Whether you believe it or not, you were, until she found out the truth."

"Mom..."

"You loved her. That's why you were so hurt. That's why you were so set on revenge. Can't you see that?"

"Mom..."

"You haven't been happy since she left, so whatever you have to do to bring Caitlyn back into your life, swallow your pride and just do it."

Judd wanted to. He really did. But... He eased

open the bottom drawer of his desk and glanced at the red shoe. Had he kept it for a reason?

Did he love her? Had he always loved her?

For a smart man, he was dangerously close to being a complete fool.

"Women like to be swept off their feet, don't they?"

Renee blinked. "What?"

"Women like romantic gestures and the Prince Charming thing. They want magic and love, right?"

"Of course. Every woman wants love—that's the most important thing."

"Did you?" He watched her face.

She wrapped her arms around her waist. "I used to dream of Jack saying, 'Renee, you're one hell of a woman and I love you like crazy.'"

"But he never did."

"No. He equated sex with love." She pointed a finger at Judd. "Don't you make that mistake."

He already had. He rose to his feet, knowing he had only one choice. "I have to see Caitlyn."

AT MIDNIGHT, Cait knew he wasn't coming. So much for that. Now she was going to lose it all.

She trudged upstairs to get clothes for tomorrow before going to the bunkhouse. The repairs on the house were coming along nicely.

The wall in the parlor was almost complete. Even that didn't cheer her.

Grabbing jeans and a shirt, she saw the red dress hanging on her closet door. On impulse she took it down and stared at it for a long time.

Why wasn't this enough?

Judd's words came back to her. Why couldn't he see they needed so much more? Slowly, she pulled off her clothes, even her boots, and slipped into the red dress. She wiggled her toes. No shoes, but she knew where one was.

She ran down the stairs to the parlor and grabbed a bottle of wine. After uncorking it, she took a sip and headed for the barn. She hoped Maddie wouldn't come looking for her.

Cait went into the barn and took down the red shoe. Clutching it and the wine in one hand, she used the other to open the gate on Red's stall. She rubbed her horse's face and sank down into the hay to say another goodbye. Tomorrow she'd have to return her.

On that thought, she took a swig of wine and slipped on the red high heel. She lifted her foot. "What do you think, Red?" She gulped a breath. "He didn't come and it hurts. I've loved this man for so long and he keeps breaking my heart. How can he do that? Men are..." She glanced up and saw Judd leaning on the gate.

"Men are what?" he asked with a devilish grin.

"Pigs," she said, her heart beating a little faster at the sight of his handsome face. "And you're late."

"I was leaving when there was a problem with one of the heifers calving. I had to wait for the vet, and it was a long painful birth."

Cait was at a loss for words, so she said the first thing that came to her mind. "I'll return Red tomorrow."

"Red is a gift. Please accept her as such."

Her eyes held his. "I can't."

"Caitie, High Five would be in the black if it hadn't been for Harland, my employee. I take full responsibility for his actions. He only did it to get back at me. You've turned the ranch around with hard work and skill." He rubbed his hand along the top of the wooden gate. "Your father should have never come up with this crazy deal."

"Sometimes I wonder why he did that." She propped the wine bottle against the stall wall.

"I have, too, but we'll never know. You deserve High Five and I'm not taking it. Isn't that what you wanted? And Red?"

She gazed up at him, the dim bulb casting enticing shadows across his angular face. She started to reach for the bottle, but realized she didn't need the wine. All she needed was that look in his dark eyes.

"No. I told you what I want."

The words hung between them.

His eyes held hers and a giddiness swept through her from the warmth she saw there. "I've been doing a lot of thinking about this thing called love, and the difference between slam-damn-good sex and love."

"You have?" She held her breath.

"Um-hmm. Trust and respect—they're important to you?"

"Yes." The word slid from her throat.

"When you were on that windmill, you trusted me. You've always trusted me and I've let you down. That day, I knew if you fell and died, my life would be over. And when your family home burned, I saw the pain in your eyes and I felt it in my gut. I wanted you to trust that I would never hurt you again. That's the main reason I can't take High Five. I can't take anything else you love."

Slowly, he opened the gate and stepped in. Red neighed and trotted out to nibble at the fresh bale of hay Cooper had brought in earlier. Judd closed the gate and Cait's giddiness turned to euphoria.

He removed his hat and knelt in front of her. His eyes darkened. "I'm not sure if I'll get this right, but I trust you, Caitie…with my heart."

She bit her lip to keep from crying out with joy, but she hadn't yet heard the words she wanted to hear.

Reaching behind him, he pulled her red high heel from his back pocket and held it out for her to slip on.

This was right. This was perfect, and she couldn't believe Judd was making such a romantic gesture. She tucked her foot into the shoe, but there was something inside and she couldn't completely get it on. No, no. The shoe had to fit. There had to be magic.

"I can't…" She squirmed and lifted the shoe to investigate. Inside she found an engagement ring—her engagement ring. The one Judd had given her fourteen years ago.

The breath left her lungs. "It's… I…"

He took the ring from her with a grin. "Slip on the shoe."

She did, gladly, and it fit perfectly. Now she waited for the magic. Judd's magic.

He lifted her trembling hand and stared into her eyes. "Caitlyn Belle, I— I…"

This time *he* was stammering and she smiled, still waiting.

He swallowed hard. "I'm no prince, but I… I love you. Will you marry me?"

The words came out in a rush, but she heard every one.

She threw herself at him, knocking him backward into the hay. "Yes. Yes. Yes!"

He cupped her face and touched his lips to hers in a stirring, sweet kiss that was powerful and binding.

"I love you, too," she whispered between featherlike kisses. "I've always loved you and I'll never stop loving you."

"Caitie." His mouth covered hers and their tongues and hands renewed a ritual they knew well. She lay half on top of him, feeling and enjoying the hardened contours of his body.

He suddenly sat up and positioned her on his lap. She wrapped her bare legs around him, picking straw from his hair. "I can't believe this," she murmured, and pressed her breasts into his chest, feeling the power of her femininity as he groaned and kissed her neck. Hot, branding kisses trailed to her cleavage.

"I've dreamed of you in this red dress." He moaned. "I've dreamed more of removing it."

She leaned slightly away and unzipped the back. "I have nothing on underneath."

A guttural sound left his throat, and Cait was beginning to think that Sky was right about feminine wiles. She could never be so uninhibited with anyone but Judd, though. As she slipped the dress down, all her inhibitions floated away.

Her breasts filled his hands and then his mouth tasted each nipple, and tingles of desire shot from her breasts to her navel and below. Judd pulled the dress over her head and tossed it on the hay.

She still sat on his lap with her legs wrapped around him, her tousled hair spread across her shoulders. His eyes glowed as he gazed at her nudity. She'd never seen that look before and she recognized exactly what it was. Love. Love shone in his eyes. There it was—the magic she craved. She needed that and had sacrificed so much for this day. It was worth every pain she had gone through. She had definitely won the prize, as Sky so aptly put it. And the prize was Judd's love.

She slowly unbuttoned his shirt. "You have too many clothes on."

"I was thinking the same thing," he said into the warmth of her neck. "And I really need to remove these jeans."

She giggled. "Yes. I'm sitting on a bulge that needs freedom."

"Don't tease." A lazy grin spread across his face as he jerked off his shirt and threw it on top of her dress. She scooted down and helped to remove his boots, then unbuttoned his jeans. He watched as she slid down his zipper and his erection thrust into her hand.

"Oh," she murmured, and before she knew it he was out of his jeans, pushing her down into the hay. The straw scratched her back, but she hardly noticed as Judd's lips found hers. The kiss was deep, hot, and her body simmered just from the touch of his naked skin against hers.

"Caitie," he moaned into her mouth.

"Yes…now…please."

He slid into her easily, as if they'd never been apart. Once again she wrapped her legs around him, drawing him deeper and deeper until fourteen years disappeared along with the heartache. Each move, each thrust bound them closer, until the world exploded into brilliant sunshine.

Her nails dug into his back as her body welcomed the much-needed release. Judd cried her name as he trembled against her, and then there was quiet—an unbelievably peaceful quiet.

Judd couldn't bear to let her go, and they lay together for a long time, just enjoying the incredible moment. They'd made love before, but not like this. Years ago it had been hot and steamy, but as soon as it was over he'd zipped his jeans and was gone. It was just sex. Now it was so much more.

Today he wanted to hold on forever—hold on to Caitie. This was love—his heart was about to pound out of his chest with it. He needed Caitlyn. Until this moment he'd never realized how much. This was living. This was loving. Every man needed this.

He sat up and pulled her into his arms. Leaning against the stall wall, he brushed her dark hair away from her face and she sighed contentedly.

"Happy?"

"Mmm." She tilted her head to look at him.

He cupped her cheek and kissed her softly. "Good. I want you to be happy."

She nestled against him. "You make me happy."

"Then we can solve all our problems. With this much love it should be simple."

She smiled. "What problems?"

"For starters, I'm a difficult man to live with. I don't open up easily. Fear of losing you once again was the only thing that got me here. And of course, I realized I'd loved you forever."

"That's not a problem," she told him.

"Then there's my mother. She lives with me and Southern Cross is her home."

"Not a problem."

"Brenda Sue works for me and I don't want to fire her, because Harvey and his family are going through a rough time."

Cait touched his cheek. "See? You care about all these people. You're just a softie underneath that stern exterior."

"You think so?"

"Who else would put up with Brenda Sue?"

"Then there's hope for me?"

"Yes, yes." She kissed him and they forgot everything for a minute.

He gently tucked her hair behind her ears again. "The wedding has to be what *you* want, without any interference from our families."

"I can handle that."

"I have no doubt. Next is High Five. It stays in the Belle family. That's the way it should be. But you, sweet lady, I want at Southern Cross with me."

"Okay." She ran her fingers through his chest hairs and lower.

He caught her hand. "Okay?"

"Yes. As your wife I should be at Southern Cross, but as part owner of High Five I will be here some, during the day, only until my sisters, Gran and I decide what to do with the ranch."

"Deal." He squeezed her. "The offer still stands about half the royalties being returned to High Five."

"I accept graciously. Thank you."

"I love you." He kissed the tip of her nose. "And we really have to stop meeting in horse stalls."

"Oh, but it's so much fun." A bubble of laughter left her throat.

He stroked her arm. "I'm sorry I botched up that second proposal. I was protecting myself."

She raised her head from his shoulder. "I know, but I love you, so I was willing to give you a third chance to get it right. And, boy, did you get it right!"

They gazed at each other and then burst out laughing as Red looked over the stall gate at them.

A loud bump sounded from the other side.

"That's Solomon. He hears my voice and wants attention."

"He's not the only one…."

She trailed a finger down Judd's nose and he grabbed it, then nibbled at the tip.

"There's only one person getting my attention tonight. And for the record, you are my prince, my prize."

He pulled her onto his lap yet again. "Ah… I like the sound of that."

After a moment, Cait said, "Maybe we should let Red have her stall."

"In a minute," Judd whispered, and leaned his face against hers.

Neither wanted to move or end this moment—this time out of time—when love had made the difference.

EPILOGUE

Two months later…

CAITLYN WAS MARRYING Judd and the whole family was playing dress-up.

She crept downstairs in her long slip to take a look at the flowers and make sure they were arranged the way she wanted.

She clasped her hands as she gazed at all the beautiful white blossoms adorning the parlor. They were perfect. Two candelabras graced the fireplace mantel, along with a huge arrangement of white roses. This was where she wanted to say her vows—in her family home, which had been completely restored. To appease Renee, the reception and dance were being held at Southern Cross.

This wedding was much smaller than the original was to be, just the way she and Judd wanted it. She chose to wear her grandmother's wedding dress, a gorgeous Italian eyelet-lace-and-silk gown that Maddie had altered to fit. Cait never knew her sister had so many domestic talents.

"What are you doing down here?" Maddie took one arm and Sky the other. "You are not supposed to see all this." They whisked her back upstairs.

Cait was so happy Sky had come home for the wedding. Her joy was complete, and watching Gran and Kira together was an even greater joy. Cait was hoping Sky would stay, especially since Maddie had decided to run High Five, with Cooper's help.

They all had a stake in the ranch, but Cait would now back away and let her sisters make the decisions. She'd never thought anything would become more important than High Five, but Judd had. He was her life now.

An hour later, she came down the stairs in her wedding dress, her nerves humming like taut wires. Maggie was behind her, holding the long train. Sky met her at the bottom and winked. "Ready?"

"Like fourteen years ready."

Sky straightened Cait's veil. "Didn't I tell you what you had to do from the start?"

"I did, and a little more—Belle style." She laughed and Maddie's "Shh" stopped her.

Maddie squeezed past Cait on the stairs. "We have to behave. This is a special day."

"I always behave," Sky said with a straight face.

The music started and their chatter stopped. Maddie and Sky kissed her. "Good luck, big sis," they chorused. Maddie handed Cait her bouquet of roses and baby's breath, and then she and Sky gathered theirs and started down the aisle.

Cait held her breath and said a silent prayer for dreams that come true. And for love.

"Here Comes the Bride" echoed through the old house. Cait turned and walked to the parlor entrance. Her eyes went directly to Judd. He looked so handsome in his tux, and he looked nervous. But happy. She started down the aisle to marry the man of her dreams.

Thirty minutes later, Mr. and Mrs. Judd Calhoun walked out of the house toward the waiting limo. Frank stood nearby, and came up to Caitlyn and handed her an envelope.

"Congratulations, Caitlyn. In case you married Judd, your father wanted me to give you this."

She stared at the envelope and started to tuck it away to read later.

"Open it," Judd whispered, his arm around her waist. With his support, she could face anything.

She stuck a manicured nail under the flap and

ripped it open. Inside was a single sheet of paper. On it was written: "Gotcha. Love, Dad."

The sneaky old devil.

He *did* know what was best for her.

* * * * *

One Belle sister has found her true love!
Shall we try for two?
Read Linda Warren's next
book in **THE BELLES OF TEXAS** *miniseries,*
MADISON'S CHILDREN,
coming October 2009, only
from Harlequin Superromance.

*Celebrate 60 years of pure reading pleasure
with Harlequin!*

To commemorate the event, Harlequin Intrigue® is thrilled to invite you to the wedding of The Colby Agency's J. T. Baxley and his bride, Eve Mattson.

That is, of course, if J.T. can find the woman who left him at the altar. Considering he's a private investigator for one of the top agencies in the country—the best of the best—that shouldn't be a problem. The real setback is that his bride isn't who she appears to be…and her mysterious past has put them both in danger.

*Enjoy an exclusive glimpse of
Debra Webb's latest addition to*
THE COLBY AGENCY:
ELITE RECONNAISSANCE DIVISION

*THE BRIDE'S SECRETS
Available August 2009
from Harlequin Intrigue®.*

The dark figures on the dock were still firing. The bullets cutting through the surface of the water without the warning boom of shots told Eve they were using silencers.

That was to her benefit. Silencers decreased the accuracy of every shot and lessened the range.

She grabbed for the rocks. Scrambled through the darkness. Bumped her knee on a boulder. Cursed.

Burrowing into the waist-deep grass, she kept low and crawled forward. Faster. Pushed harder. Needed as much distance as possible.

Shots pinged on the rocks.

J.T. scrambled alongside her.

He was breathing hard.

They had to stay close to the ground until they reached the next row of warehouses. Even though she was relatively certain they were out of range at this point, she wasn't taking any risks. And she wasn't slowing down.

J.T. had to keep up.

The splat of a bullet hitting the ground next to Eve had her rolling left. Maybe they weren't completely out of range.

She bumped J.T. He grunted.

His injured arm. Dammit. She could apologize later.

Half a dozen more yards.

Almost in the clear.

As she reached the cover of the alley between the first two warehouses she tensed.

Silence.

No pings or splats.

She glanced back at the dock. Deserted.

Time to run.

Her car was parked another block down.

Pushing to her feet, she sprinted forward. The wet bag dragged at her shoulder. She ignored it.

By the time she reached the lot where her car was parked, she had dug the keys from her pocket and hit the fob. Six seconds later she was behind the wheel. She hit the ignition as J.T. collapsed into the passenger seat. Tires squealed as she spun out of the slot.

"What the hell did you do to me?"

From the corner of her eye she watched him shake his head in an attempt to clear it.

He would be pissed when she told him about the tranquilizer.

She'd needed him cooperative until she formulated a plan. A drug-induced state of unconsciousness had been the fastest and most efficient method to ensure his continued solidarity.

"I can't really talk right now." Eve weaved into the right lane as the street widened to four lanes. What she needed was traffic. It was Saturday night—shouldn't be that difficult to find as soon as they were out of the old warehouse district.

A glance in the rearview mirror warned that their unwanted company had caught up.

Sensing her tension, J.T. turned to peer over his left shoulder.

"I hope you have a plan B."

She shot him a look. "There's always plan G." Then she pulled the Glock out of her waistband.

Cutting the steering wheel left, she slid between two vehicles. Another veer to the right and she'd put several cars between hers and the enemy.

She was betting they wouldn't pull out the firepower in the open like this, but a girl could never be too sure when it came to an unknown enemy.

Deep blending was the way to go.

Two traffic lights ahead, the marquis of a movie theater provided exactly the opportunity she was looking for.

The digital numbers on the dash indicated it was just past midnight. Perfect timing. The late movie would be purging its audience into the crowd of teenagers who liked hanging out in the parking lot.

She took a hard right onto the property that sported a twelve-screen theater, numerous fast-food hot spots and a chain superstore. Speeding across the lot, she selected a lane of parking slots. Pulling in as close to the theater entrance as possible, she shut off the engine and reached for her door.

"Let's go."

Thankfully he didn't argue.

Rounding the hood of her car, she shoved the Glock into her bag, then wrapped her arm around J.T.'s and merged into the crowd.

With her free hand, she finger-combed her long hair. It was soaked, as were her clothes. The kids she bumped into noticed, gave her death-ray glares.

They just didn't know.

As she and J.T. moved in closer to the building, she grabbed a baseball cap from an innocent by-stander. The crowd made it easy. The kid who owned the cap had made it even easier by stuffing the cap bill-first into his waistband at the small of his back.

Pushing through the loitering crowd, she made her way to the side of the building next to the main entrance. She pushed J.T. against the wall and dropped her bag to the ground. Peeled off her T-shirt and let it fall.

His gaze instantly zeroed in on her breasts, where the cami she wore had glued to her skin like an extra layer. A zing of desire shot through her veins.

Not the time.

With a flick of her wrist she twisted her hair up and clamped the cap atop the blond mass.

"They're coming," J.T. muttered as he gazed at some point beyond her.

"Yeah, I know." She planted her palms against the wall on either side of him and leaned in. "Keep your eyes open. Let me know when they're inside."

Then she planted her lips on his.

* * * * *

Will J.T. and Eve be caught in the moment?
Or will Eve get the chance to reveal
all of her secrets?
Find out in
THE BRIDE'S SECRETS
by Debra Webb.
Available August 2009
from Harlequin Intrigue®.

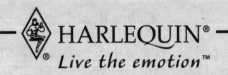

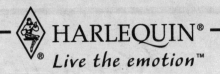

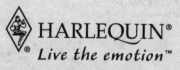

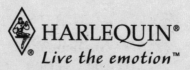

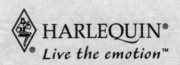

Harlequin® Historical
Historical Romantic Adventure!

Imagine a time of chivalrous knights and unconventional ladies, roguish rakes and impetuous heiresses, rugged cowboys and spirited frontierswomen— these rich and vivid tales will capture your imagination!

Harlequin Historical . . . they're too good to miss!

SPECIAL EDITION™

Emotional, compelling stories that capture the intensity of living, loving and creating a family in today's world.

Silhouette Desire

Modern, passionate reads that are powerful and provocative.

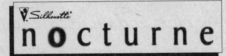

Dramatic and sensual tales of paranormal romance.

Romances that are sparked by danger and fueled by passion.

SDIR07